The Rebellion
of Young David
and Other Stories

The Rebellion
of Young David
and Other Stories
by Ernest Buckler

Selected and arranged by Robert D. Chambers,
Department of English Literature, Trent University.

McClelland and Stewart Limited

ISBN 0-7710-1766-9

McClelland and Stewart Limited
The Canadian Publishers
25 Hollinger Road, Toronto

Acknowledgment is gratefully made to the following periodicals
for permission to reprint these short stories:

Atlantic Advocate for—
The Wild Goose (October 1959)
Long, Long After School (November 1959)
Cleft Rock, With Spring (October 1957)
Glance in the Mirror (January 1957)

Chatelaine for—
The Dream and the Triumph (November 1956)
A Present for Miss Merriam (December 1952)
Last Delivery Before Christmas (December 1953)

Esquire for—
The First Born Son (July 1941)

Maclean's for—
Penny in the Dust (December 15, 1948)
The Rebellion of Young David (November 15, 1951)
The Quarrel (January 15, 1949)
The Clumsy One (August 1, 1950)

Saturday Night for—
Another Christmas (December 20, 1941)
You Could Go Anywhere Now (November 2, 1946)

Printed and bound in Canada
by
John Deyell Company

Contents

*FATHERS
AND SONS*

Penny in the Dust

My sister and I were walking through the old sun-still fields the evening before my father's funeral, recalling this memory or that—trying, after the fashion of families who gather again in the place where they were born, to identify ourselves with the strange children we must have been.

"Do you remember the afternoon we thought you were lost?" my sister said. I did. That was as long ago as the day I was seven, but I'd had occasion to remember it only yesterday.

"We searched everywhere," she said. "Up in the meeting-house, back in the blueberry barrens—we even looked in the well. I think it's the only time I ever saw Father really upset. He didn't even stop to take the oxen off the wagon tongue when they told him. He raced right through the chopping where Tom Reeve was burning brush, looking for you—right through the flames almost; they couldn't do a thing with him. And you up in your bed, sound asleep!"

"It was all over losing a penny or something, wasn't it?" she went on, when I didn't answer. It was. She laughed indulgently. "You were a crazy kid, weren't you."

I was. But there was more to it than that. I had never seen a shining new penny before that day. I'd thought they were all black. This one was bright as gold. And my father had given it to me.

You would have to understand about my father, and that is the hard thing to tell. If I say that he worked all day long but never once had I seen him hurry, that would make him sound like a stupid man. If I say that he never held me on his knee when I was a child and that I never heard him laugh out loud in his life, it would make him sound humourless and severe. If I said that whenever I'd be reeling off some of my fanciful plans and he'd come into the kitchen and I'd stop short, you'd think that he was

3

distant and that in some kind of way I was afraid of him. None of that would be true.

There's no way you can tell it to make it sound like anything more than an inarticulate man a little at sea with an imaginative child. You'll have to take my word for it that there was more to it than that. It was as if his sure-footed way in the fields forsook him the moment he came near the door of my child's world and that he could never intrude on it without feeling awkward and conscious of trespass; and that I, sensing that but not understanding it, felt at the sound of his solid step outside, the child-world's foolish fragility. He would fix the small spot where I planted beans and other quick-sprouting seeds before he prepared the big garden, even if the spring was late; but he wouldn't ask me how many rows I wanted and if he made three rows and I wanted four, I couldn't ask him to change them. If I walked behind the load of hay, longing to ride, and he walked ahead of the oxen, I couldn't ask him to put me up and he wouldn't make any move to do so until he saw me trying to grasp the binder.

He, my father, had just given me a new penny, bright as gold.

He'd taken it from his pocket several times, pretending to examine the date on it, waiting for me to notice it. He couldn't offer me *anything* until I had shown some sign that the gift would be welcome.

"You can have it if you want it, Pete," he said at last.

"Oh, thanks," I said. Nothing more. I couldn't expose any of my eagerness either.

I started with it, to the store. For a penny you could buy the magic cylinder of "Long Tom" popcorn with Heaven knows what glittering bauble inside. But the more I thought of my bright penny disappearing forever into the black drawstring pouch the storekeeper kept his money in, the slower my steps lagged as the store came nearer and nearer. I sat down in the road.

It was that time of magic suspension in an August afternoon. The lifting smells of leaves and cut clover hung still in the sun. The sun drowsed, like a kitten curled up on my shoulder. The deep flour-fine dust in the road puffed about my bare ankles, warm and soft as sleep. The sound of the cowbells came sharp and hollow from the cool swamp.

I began to play with the penny, putting off the decision. I would close my eyes and bury it deep in the sand; and then, with my eyes still closed, get up and walk around, and then come back to search for it. Tantalizing myself, each time, with the excitement of discovering afresh its bright shining edge. I did that again and again. Alas, once too often.

It was almost dark when their excited talking in the room awakened me. It was Mother who had found me. I suppose when it came dusk she thought of me in my bed other nights, and I suppose she looked there without any reasonable hope but only as you look in every place where the thing that is lost has ever lain before. And now suddenly she was crying because when she opened the door there, miraculously, I was.

"Peter!" she cried, ignoring the obvious in her sudden relief, "*where* have you been?"

"I lost my penny," I said.

"You lost your penny . . . ? But what made you come up here and hide?"

If Father hadn't been there, I might have told her the whole story. But when I looked up at Father, standing there like the shape of everything sound and straight, it was like daylight shredding the memory of a silly dream. How could I bear the shame of repeating before him the childish visions I had built in my head in the magic August afternoon when almost anything could be made to seem real, as I buried the penny and dug it up again? How could I explain that pit-of-the-stomach sickness which struck through the whole day when I had to believe, at last, that it was really gone? How could I explain that I wasn't really hiding from *them*? How, with the words and the understanding I had then, that this was the only possible place to run from that awful feeling of loss?

"I lost my penny," I said again. I looked at Father and turned my face into the pillow. "I want to go to sleep."

"Peter," Mother said. "It's almost nine o'clock. You haven't had a bite of supper. Do you know you almost scared the *life* out of us?"

"You better get some supper," Father said. It was the only time he had spoken.

I never dreamed that he would mention the thing again. But the next morning when we had the hay forks in our hands, ready to toss out the clover, he seemed to postpone the moment of actually leaving for the field. He stuck his fork in the ground and brought in another pail of water, though the kettle was chock full.

5

He took out the shingle nail that held a broken yoke strap together and put it back in exactly the same hole. He went into the shed to see if the pigs had cleaned up all their breakfast.

And then he said abruptly: "Ain't you got no idea where you lost your penny?"

"Yes," I said, "I know just about."

"Let's see if we can't find it," he said.

We walked down the road together, stiff with awareness. He didn't hold my hand.

"It's right here somewhere," I said. "I was playin' with it, in the dust."

He looked at me, but he didn't ask me what game anyone could possibly play with a penny in the dust.

I might have known he would find it. He could tap the alder bark with his jackknife just exactly hard enough so it wouldn't split but so it would twist free from the notched wood, to make a whistle. His great fingers could trace loose the hopeless snarl of a fishing line that I could only succeed in tangling tighter and tighter. If I broke the handle of my wheelbarrow ragged beyond sight of any possible repair, he could take it and bring it back to me so you could hardly see the splice if you weren't looking for it.

He got down on his knees and drew his fingers carefully through the dust, like a harrow; not clawing it frantically into heaps as I had done, covering even as I uncovered. He found the penny almost at once.

He held it in his hand, as if the moment of passing it to me were a deadline for something he dreaded to say, but must. Something that could not be put off any longer, if it were to be spoken at all.

"Pete," he said, "you needn'ta hid. I wouldn'ta beat you."

Beat me? Oh, Father! You didn't think that was the reason . . . ? I felt almost sick. I felt as if I had struck *him*.

I had to tell him the truth then. Because only the truth, no matter how ridiculous it was, would have the unmistakable sound truth has, to scatter that awful idea out of his head.

"I wasn't hidin', Father," I said, "honest. I was. . . . I was buryin' my penny and makin' out I was diggin' up treasure. I was makin' out I was findin' gold. I didn't know what to *do* when I lost it, I just didn't know where to *go*. . . ." His head was bent forward, like mere listening. I had to make it truer still.

"I made out it was gold," I said desperately, "and I—I was

makin' out I bought you a mowin' machine so's you could get your
work done early every day so's you and I could go in to town in the
big automobile I made out I bought you—and everyone'd turn
around and look at us drivin' down the streets. . . ." His head was
perfectly still, as if he were only waiting with patience for me to
finish. "*Laughin'* and *talkin'*," I said. Louder, smiling intensely,
com*pell*ing him, by the absolute conviction of some true particular, to believe me.

He looked up then. It was the only time I had ever seen tears
in his eyes. It was the only time in my seven years that he had ever
put his arm around me.

I wondered, though, why he hesitated, and then put the
penny back in his own pocket.

Yesterday I knew. I never found any fortune and we never
had a car to ride in together. But I think he knew what that would
be like, just the same. I found the penny again yesterday, when
we were getting out his good suit—in an upper vest pocket where
no one ever carries change. It was still shining. He must have
kept it polished.

I left it there.

The Rebellion
of Young David

There are times when you can only look at your son and say his
name over and over in your mind.

I would say, "David, David. . ." nights when he was
asleep—the involuntary way you pass your hand across your eyes
when your head aches, though there is no way for your hand to
get inside. It seemed as if it must all have been my fault.

I suppose any seven-year-old has a look of accusing in-
nocence when he is asleep, an assaulting grudgelessness. But it
seemed to me that he had it especially. It seemed incredible that
when I'd told him to undress he'd said, "You make me!" his eyes
dark and stormy. It seemed incredible that those same legs and

hands, absolutely pliant now, would ever be party to that isolating violence of his again.

His visible flesh was still; yet he was always moving in a dream. Maybe he'd cry, "Wait. . . . Wait up, Art." Where was I going in the dream, what was I doing, that even as I held him in my arms he was falling behind?

He called me "Art," not "Dad." The idea was: we were pals.

I had never whipped him. The thought of my wife—who died when David was born—had something to do with that, I guess. And a curious suggestion of vulnerability about his wire-thin body, his perceptive face, so contrasted with its actual belligerence that the thought of laying a hand on him—well, I just couldn't do it. We were supposed to *reason* things out.

Sometimes that worked. Sometimes it didn't.

He *could* reason, as well as I. His body would seem to vibrate with obedience. His friendship would be absolutely unwithholding. "You stepped on my hand," he'd say, laughing, though his face was pinched with the pain of it, "but that doesn't matter, does it, Art? Sometimes you can't see people's hands when they stick them in the way." Or if we were fishing, he'd say, "You tell me when to pull on the line, won't you, Art . . . just right *when*."

Then, without any warning whatever, he'd become possessed by this automatic inaccessible mutiny.

I'd get the awful feeling then that we were both lost. That whatever I'd done wrong had not only failed, but that he'd never know I'd been *trying* to do it right for him. Worse still, that his mind was rocked by some blind contradiction he'd never understand himself.

Maybe I'd be helping him with a reading lesson. I tried to make a game of it, totalling the words he named right against words he named wrong. He'd look at me, squinting up his face into a contortion of deliberate ingratiation. He'd say, "Seventeen right and only one wrong . . . wouldn't that make you *laugh*, Art?" Then maybe the very next word I'd ask him, he'd slump against the table in a pretended indolence; or flop the book shut while the smile was still on my face.

Or maybe we'd be playing with his new baseball bat and catcher's mitt.

His hands were too small to grasp the bat properly and his fingers were lost in the mitt. But he couldn't have seemed more obliteratingly happy when he did connect with the ball. ("Boy, that was a solid hit, wasn't it, Art? You throw them to me *just* right, Art, just *right.*") He'd improvise rules of his own for the game. His face would twist with the delight of communicating them to me.

Then, suddenly, when he'd throw the ball, he'd throw it so hard that the physical smart of it on my bare fingers would sting me to exasperation.

"All right," I'd say coolly, "if you don't want to play, I'll go hoe the garden."

I'd go over to the garden, watching him out of the corner of my eye. He'd wander forlornly about the yard. Then I'd see him coming slowly toward the garden (where his tracks still showed along the top of a row of carrots he'd raced through yesterday). He'd come up behind me and say, "I have to walk right between the rows, don't I? Gardens are hard *work*, aren't they, Art . . . you don't want anyone stepping on the rows."

David, David. . . .

The strange part, it wasn't that discipline had no effect because it made no impression.

One evening he said out of a blue sky, "*You're* so smart, Art . . . I haven't got a brain in my head, not one. You've got so many *brains*, Art, *brains*. . . ." I was completely puzzled.

Then I remembered: I had countered with complete silence when he'd called me "dumb" that morning. I'd forgotten the incident entirely. But he hadn't. Though he'd been less rather than more tractable since then, he'd been carrying the snub around with him all day.

Or take the afternoon there was only one nickel in his small black purse. I saw him take it out and put it back again several times before he came and asked me for another. He never asked me for money unless he wanted it terribly. I gave him another nickel. He went to the store and came back with two Cokes. For some reason he had to treat me.

My face must have shown my gratification. He said, with his devastating candour, "You look happier with me than you did this morning, don't you, Art?"

I couldn't even recall the offence that time. *He* had felt my displeasure, though on my part it must have been quite unconscious.

What had I done wrong? I didn't know.

Unless it was that, when he was small, I'd kept a harness on him in the yard. He rebelled, instinctively, at any kind of bond. But what else could I do? Our house was on a blind corner. What else could I do, when I had the picture of the strength of his slight headlong body falling against the impersonal strength of a truck, or the depth of a well?

David, David. . . .

I said, "David, David . . ." out loud, that particular afternoon he lay so still on the ground; because this is the way it had happened.

I had taken him fencing with me that morning. It was one of those perfect spring mornings when even the woods seem to breathe out a clean water-smell. He was very excited. He'd never been to the back of the pasture before.

I carried the axe and the mall. He carried the staple-box and the two hammers. Sometimes he walked beside me, sometimes ahead.

There was something about him that always affected me when I watched him moving *back to*. I'd made him wear his rubber boots because there was a swamp to cross. Now the sun was getting hot. I wished I'd let him wear his sneakers and carried him across the swamp. There was something about the heavy boots *not* slowing up his eager movement and the thought that they must be tiring him without his consciousness of it.

I asked him if his legs weren't tired. "Noooooo," he scoffed. As if that were the kind of absurd question people kid each other with to clinch the absolute perfection of the day. Then he added, "If your legs do get a little tired when you're going some place, that doesn't hurt, does it, Art?"

His unpredictable twist of comment made him good company, in an adult way. Yet there was no unnatural shadow of precocity about him. His face had a kind of feature-smalling brightness that gave him a peaked look when he was tired or disappointed, and when his face was washed and the water on his hair, for town, a kind of shining. But it was as childlike and unwithholding as the clasp of his hand. (Or maybe he didn't look much different from any other child. Maybe I couldn't see him straight because I loved him.)

This was one of his days of intense, jubilant, communicativeness. One of his "How come?" days. As if by his questions and my answers we (and we alone) could find out about everything.

If I said anything mildly funny he worked himself up into quite a glee. I knew his laughter was a little louder than natural.

His face would twitch a little, renewing it, each time I glanced at him. But that didn't mean that his amusement was false. I knew that his intense willingness to think anything funny I said was as funny as anything could possibly be, tickled him more than the joke itself. "You always say such funny things, Art!"

We came to the place where I had buried the horse. Dogs had dug away the earth. The brackets of its ribs and the chalky grimace of its jaws stared whitely in the bright sun.

He looked at it with a sudden quietness beyond mere attention; as if something invisible were threatening to come too close. I thought he was a little pale. He had never seen a skeleton before.

"Those bones can't move, *can* they, Art?" he said.

"No," I said.

"How can bones move?"

"Oh, they have to have flesh on them, and muscles, and. . . ."

"Well, could he move when he was just dead? I mean right then, when he was right just dead?"

"No."

"How come?"

I was searching for a reply when he moved very close to me. "Could you carry the hammers, Art, please?" he said.

I put the hammers in my back overalls pocket.

"Could *you* carry an axe and a mall both in one hand?" he said.

I took the axe in my left hand, with the mall, so that now we each had a hand free. He took my hand and tugged me along the road.

He was quiet for a few minutes, then he said, "Art? What goes away out of your muscles when you're dead?"

He was a good boy all morning. He was really a help. If you fence alone you can't carry all the tools through the brush at once. You have to replace a stretch of rotted posts with the axe and mall; then return to where you've left the staple-box and hammers and go over the same ground again, tightening the wire.

He carried the staple-box and hammers and we could complete the operation as we went. He held the wire taut while I drove the staples. He'd get his voice down very low. "The way you do it, Art, see, you get the claw of your hammer right behind a barb so it won't slip . . . so it won't *slip*, Art, see?" As if he'd

11

discovered some trick that would now be a conspiratorial secret between just us two. The obbligato of manual labour was like a quiet stitching together of our presences.

We started at the far end of the pasture and worked toward home. It was five minutes past eleven when we came within sight of the skeleton again. The spot where my section of the fence ended. That was fine. We could finish the job before noon and not have to walk all the way back again after dinner. It was aggravating when I struck three rotten posts in a row; but we could still finish, if we hurried. I thought David looked a little pale again.

"You take off those heavy boots and rest, while I go down to the intervale and cut some posts," I said. There were no trees growing near the fence.

"All right, Art." He was very quiet. There was that look of suspension in his flesh he'd get sometimes when his mind was working on something it couldn't quite manoeuvre.

It took me no more than twenty minutes to cut the posts, but when I carried them back to the fence he wasn't there.

"Bring the staples, chum," I shouted. He didn't pop out from behind any bush.

"David! David!" I called, louder. There was only that hollow stillness of the wind rustling the leaves when you call to someone in the woods and there is no answer. He had completely disappeared.

I felt a sudden irritation. Of all the damn times to beat it home without telling me!

I started to stretch the wire alone. But an uneasiness began to insinuate itself. Anyone could follow that wide road home. But what if . . . I didn't know just what . . . but what if something . . . ? Oh dammit, I'd have to go find him.

I kept calling him all the way along the road. There was no answer. How could he get out of sound so quickly, unless he ran? He must have run all the way. But why? I began to run, myself.

My first reaction when I saw him standing by the house, looking toward the pasture, was intense relief. Then, suddenly my irritation was compounded.

He seemed to sense my annoyance, even from a distance. He began to wave, as if in propitiation. He had a funny way of waving, holding his arm out still and moving his hand up and down very slowly. I didn't wave back. When I came close enough that he could see my face he stopped waving.

"I thought you'd come home without me, Art," he said.

"Why should you think that?" I said, very calmly.

He wasn't defiant as I'd expected him to be. He looked as if he were relieved to see me; but as if at the sight of me coming from that direction he knew he'd done something wrong. Now he was trying to pass the thing off as an amusing quirk in the way things had turned out. Though half-suspecting that this wouldn't go over. His tentative over-smiling brushed at my irritation, but didn't dislodge it.

"I called to you, Art," he said.

I just looked at him, as much as to say, do you think I'm deaf?

"Yes, I called. I thought you'd come home some other way."

"Now I've got to traipse all the way back there this afternoon to finish one rod of fence," I said.

"I thought you'd gone and left me," he said.

I ignored him, and walked past him into the house.

He didn't eat much dinner, but he wasn't defiant about that, either, as he was, sometimes, when he refused to eat. And after dinner he went out and sat down on the banking, by himself. He didn't know that his hair was sticking up through the heart-shaped holes in the skullcap with all the buttons pinned on it.

When it was time to go back to the woods again he hung around me with his new bat and ball. Tossing the ball up himself and trying to hit out flies.

"Boy, you picked out the very best bat there was, didn't you, Art?" he said. I knew he thought I'd toss him a few. I didn't pay any attention to what he was doing.

When I started across the yard, he said, "Do you want me to carry the axe this afternoon? That makes it *easier* for you, doesn't it, Art?"

"I'll be back in an hour or so," I said. "You play with Max."

He went as far as the gate with me. Then he stopped. I didn't turn around. It sounds foolish, but everything between us was on such an adult basis that it wasn't until I bent over to crawl through the barbed wire fence that I stole a glance at him, covertly. He was tossing the ball up again and trying to hit it. It always fell to the ground, because the bat was so unwieldy and because he had one eye on me.

I noticed he still had on his hot rubber boots. I had intended to change them for his sneakers. He was the sort of child who seems unconsciously to invest his clothes with his own mood. The thought of his clothes, when he was forlorn, struck me as hard as the thought of his face.

Do you know the kind of thoughts you have when you go back alone to a job which you have been working at happily with another? When that work together has ended in a quarrel . . . with your accusations unprotested, and, after that, your rejection of his overtures unprotested too?

I picked up my tools and began to work. But I couldn't seem to work quickly.

I'd catch myself, with the hammer slack in my hands, thinking about crazy things like his secret pride in the new tie (which he left outside his pullover until he saw that the other children had theirs inside) singling him so abatedly from the town children, the Saturday I took him to the matinee, that I felt an unreasonable rush of protectiveness toward him. . . . Of him laughing dutifully at the violence in the comedy, but crouching a little toward me, while the other children, who were not nearly so violent as he, shrieked together in a seizure of delight.

I thought of his scribblers, with the fixity there of the letters which his small hand had formed earnestly, but awry.

I thought of those times when the freak would come upon him to recount all his trangressions of the day, insisting on his guilt with phrases of my own I had never expected him to remember.

I thought of him playing ball with the other children.

At first they'd go along with the outlandish variations he'd introduce into the game, because it was his equipment. Then, somehow, *they'd* be playing with the bat and glove and he'd be out of it, watching.

I thought now of him standing there, saying, "Boy, I hope my friends come to play with me early tomorrow, *early*, Art"—though I knew that if they came at all their first question would be, "Can we use your bat and glove?"

I thought of him asleep. I thought, if anything should ever happen to him that's the way he would look.

I laughed; to kid myself for being such a soft and sentimental fool. But it was no use. The feeling came over me, immediate as the sound of a voice, that someting *was* happening to him right now.

14

It was coincidence, of course, but I don't believe that . . . because I had started to run even before I came over the crest of the knoll by the barn. Before I saw the cluster of excited children by the horse stable.

I couldn't see David among them, but I saw the ladder against the roof. I saw Max running toward the stable, with my neighbour running behind him. I knew, by the way the children looked at me—with that half-discomfited awe that was always in their faces whenever any recklessness of David's was involved —what had happened.

"He fell off the roof," one of them said.

I held him, and I said, "David, David. . . ."

He stirred. "Wait," he said drowsily, "Wait up, Art. . . ."

I suppose it's foolish to think that if I hadn't been right there, right then, to call his name, he would never have come back. Because he was only stunned. The doctor could scarcely find a bruise on him. (I don't know just why my eyes stung when the doctor patted his head in admiration of his patience, when the exhaustive examination was over. He was always so darned quiet and brave at the doctor's and dentist's.)

I read to him the rest of the afternoon. He'd sit quiet all day, with the erasure on his face as smooth as the erasure of sleep, if you read to him.

After supper, I decided to finish the fence. It was the season of long days.

"Do you want to help me finish the fence?" I said. I thought he'd be delighted.

"No," he said. "You go on. I'll wait right here. Right here, Art."

"Who's going to help me stretch the wire?" I said.

"All right," he said.

He scarcely spoke until we got almost back to the spot where the skeleton was. Then he stopped and said, "We better go back, Art. It's going to be dark."

"G'way with ya," I said. "It won't be dark for hours." It wouldn't be although the light *was* an eerie after-supper light.

"I'm going home," he said. His voice and his face were suddenly defiant.

"You're not going home," I said sharply. "Now come on, hurry up."

I was carrying an extra pound of staples I had picked up in

town that afternoon. He snatched the package from my hand. Before I could stop him he broke the string and strewed them far and wide.

I suppose I was keyed up after the day, for I did then what I had never done before. I took him and held him and I put it onto him, hard and thoroughly.

He didn't try to escape. For the first few seconds he didn't make a sound. The only retraction of his defiance was a kind of crouching in his eyes when he first realized what I was going to do. Then he began to cry. He cried and cried.

"You're *going* home," I said, "and you're going right to *bed*."

I could see the marks of my fingers on his bare legs, when I undressed him. He went to sleep almost immediately. But though it was perfectly quiet downstairs for reading, the words of my book might have been any others.

When I got him up to the toilet, he had something to say, as usual. But this time he was wide awake. I sat down on the side of his bed for a minute.

"Bones make you feel funny, don't they, Art?" was what he said.

I remembered then.

I remembered that the skeleton was opposite the place where he sat down to rest. I remembered how he had shrunk from it on the way back. I remembered then that the wind had been blowing *away* from me, when I was cutting the posts. That's why I hadn't heard him call. I thought of him calling, and then running along the road alone, in the heavy, hot, rubber boots.

David, David, I thought, do I always fail you like that? . . . the awful misinterpretation a child has to endure! I couldn't answer him.

"I thought you'd gone home, Art," he said.

"I'm sorry," I said. I couldn't seem to find any words to go on with.

"I'm sorry too I threw the staples," he said eagerly.

"I'm sorry I spanked you."

"No, no," he said. "You spank me every time I do that, won't you, Dad? . . . *spank* me, Dad."

His night-face seemed happier than I had ever seen it. As if the trigger-spring of his driving restlessness had been finally cut.

I won't say it came in a flash. It wasn't such a simple thing as that. But could that be what I had done wrong?

He had called me "Dad." Could it be that a child would rather have a father than a pal? ("Wait. . . . Wait up, Art.") By spanking him I had abrogated the adult partnership between us and set him free. He could cry. His guilt could be paid for all at once and absolved.

It wasn't the spanking that had been cruel. What had been cruel were all the times I had snubbed him as you might an adult—with implication of shame. There was no way he could get over that. The unexpiable residue of blame piled up in him. Shutting him out, spreading (who can tell what unlikely symptoms a child's mind will translate it into?), blocking his access to me, to other children, even to himself. His reaction was violence, deviation. Any guilt a sensitive child can't be absolved of at once he blindly adds to, whenever he thinks of it, in a kind of desperation.

I had worried about failing him. That hadn't bothered him. What had bothered him was an adult shame I had taught him, I saw now, for failing *me*.

I kissed him good-night. "Okay, son," I said, "I'll spank you sometimes."

He nodded, smiling. "Dad," he said then, "how come you knew I jumped off the roof?"

That should have brought me up short—how much farther apart we must be than I'd imagined if he was driven to jump off a roof to shock me back into contact. "Jumped," he said, not "fell."

But somehow it didn't. It gave me the most liberating kind of hope. Because it hadn't been a question, really. It had been a statement. "How come you *knew* . . . ?" He hadn't the slightest doubt that no matter what he did, wherever I was I would know it, and that wherever I was I would come.

Anyhow, it is a fine day today, and we have just finished the fence. He is playing ball with the other children as I put this down. Their way.

The First Born Son

The pale cast of fatigue smudged Martin's skin and little grooves of it emptied into the corners of his mouth. But this land was his own, and a son of his own flesh was holding the plough that broke it. His thoughts were tired half-thoughts but they did not ache.

He felt the wine of the fall day and for a minute his feet wandered, inattentive, from the furrow. The dogged, slow-eyed oxen followed him, straining nose-down at his heels. The plough ran out wide in the sod. David tried to flip over the furrow with a sudden wrench of the handles, but the chocolate-curling lip of earth broke and the share came clear.

"Whoa!" David yelled.

"Whoa!" Martin roared at the oxen.

"For God's sake, Dad, can't you watch where you're going? It's hard enough to hold this damn thing when you keep 'em straight."

"Now don't get high," Martin said. But there was no echo of David's temper in his voice. He knew David was tired. And David could not learn to handle his weariness. He fought it. It was no use to do that. If you let it come and go, quietly, after supper it made a lazy song in your muscles and was good to think about. Martin remembered the night David was born. They had thought Ellen would die. It was Christmas Eve. There was not a breath of wind in the moonlit, Christmas-kindled air. Snow lay in kind folds on the ground, shadowed in the dead-still moonlight like the wrinkles of a white cloak. On the brook Martin could watch the gay, meaningless movements of the children skating. And sometimes a fragment of their heartless laughter would break away and fall inside the room. Ellen's pain-tight face stared at her pale hands outside the quilt. The kind-smelling Christmas tree was a cruel mockery. Now and then Martin would go outside and listen, bare-headed, for the doctor's sleighbells, trying to separate their faint, far-off tinkle from the frost-crackle of the spruces. He would think he heard them. Then there would be nothing. Runner tracks shone like ising-glass in the moonlight. He heard nothing but the heartless laughter of the children.

It seemed hours later, when he was not listening at all, that he looked out and all at once the dark body of the horse turned in the gate, by the corner of the house. His heart gave a great leap. The helplessness left him. This man could hold Ellen back from death. The moonlight seemed to turn warm. After the doctor went in with Ellen the laughing of the children did not seem so far-off and strange.

The quick white grip of fear came again when he heard the doctor's hand on the door again . . . but Martin looked up and the doctor was *smiling*. Suddenly the whole night was a great, neighbourly, tear-starting friend. He had a son now. He knew it would be a son.

Martin felt shy to kiss Ellen in front of the doctor, but there was a new peace and a strange swagger in his soul. When he got the doctor's horse for him, it seemed like the best horse in all the world; and half-ashamed and half-afraid not to, but somehow wanting desperately to thank *someone*, he knelt down for a minute on the hay and prayed. Outside the barn, the voices of the children laughing were a glad song in his ears, now. In the bedroom, Ellen murmured "My own little Jesus". . . and the thick spruce-cosy smell of the Christmas tree and the shining moonlight outside and the soft peace after danger past clothed the minutes in a sweet armour. . . . A son. . . . A son. . . . And Ellen well. . . . Martin couldn't believe how good it was. He would never die now. He had a son, now . . . when he was too old to break up the land he loved, any more, this son would come in at night and they would plan together, just the same. This son's sons. . . .

"Well, maybe you think it's *easy* to hold this damn thing," David said. It *must* be that he's tired, Martin thought. He can't mean that . . . this same David . . . my own son cannot find it hard to plough this land of our own. I never found it so, when I was young. Ploughed land was always the prettiest sight in the world to me. It was always good at the end of the day, to stand and look over the brown waves of earth and know that I had opened my land to the sun and the air and the rain. I don't like to hear this son of mine talk that way. He says too many things like that. I don't like to hear my son talk that way. The ploughed land was here before us and it will last after us and our hands should be proud to work in it.

"Haw," Martin called, and the lip of the earth curled back and buried the grass again.

In the city, David thought, their bodies are not dead-tired now. They have not walked all day in their own tracks . . . back and forth, back and forth, in their own damn tracks. There is movement and lights and laughing. Every day there is something *new* . . . something to keep alive for. The same people here . . . the same talk . . . the same eternal drudgery . . . your nose in the ground all day long, from morning till night, like a damned ox . . . cooped up in that damned circle of trees.

The last brown beech leaves on the hardwood hill drifted down to the ground, dreamily, a little sad to die. A flock of partridges made their heavy headlong flight into an apple tree and began to bud. In the fields, the potato stalks lay in blackened heaps. The earth was grey and brown. All the colour was in the sky or hung in the thin air. Only the stray pumpkins, left to ripen on the withered vines, gave back any of it. They were like bubbles of the sad October sunshine. Martin loved these quick chill dusks, and then later the kind eye of lamplight in the window, and the friendly, wood-warmed, table-set kitchen.

They came to the end of the furrow. Martin split the rest of the acre with his eye.

"Will we finish her before supper, son?" he asked.

"Do you want to work all night too!"

Martin stopped the oxen.

"What's wrong with you today, Dave?" he said. "If you planned to go after the partridges. . . ."

"Partridges, hell!"

"Well then, what's. . . ."

David hesitated.

"I'm so damn sick of this place I. . . ."

"Is *that* so!" Martin said slowly. "What's wrong with this place?" He kicked over a sod with the toe of his shabby boot. An old man looked out of his face for the first time. It was true, then. . . . It had never been because David was tired or lonely or weak or young. . . . It was because David had always *hated* this land . . . the land that would be his own some day. A sick little cloud settled on his heart. He *had* no son, then.

"What's *wrong* with it?" David said. "The same damn thing over and over from morning till night . . . every day and every day . . . what future is there for anyone here?" David kept his back

20

bent to the plough handles. He felt a little mean and ashamed when he heard the sound of his own words.

"What future is there here?" The question sounded meaningless to Martin. He had the truth, to contradict it. There is the first day in April when the fields stir again and it is good all day just to feel your breathing. . . . There is the sky-blue August day when the whole green wind is full of leaves and growing, and Sunday morning you walk in the waving growth-full garden rows and wish you could keep this day forever, hold it back from going. . . . It is good, too, when the snow whistles cold and mournful because it can never get inside the pane to warm itself. . . . It is *all* good, all of it. . . . Men live here as long as their sons live, to see the clearings their axes have made and the living grass that sprang from their tracks in the first furrow and the green things their hands gave life to. . . . "The same thing over and over. . . ." Martin did not speak. Only his sick thoughts pleaded, patiently, silently, incredulously. We did not plough yesterday, David. We took the day off and last night this time we sat at the edge of the woods and waited for the shy-eyed deer to come out into the old back field.

I thought it was good to sit there and smoke with my son after we boiled the supper kettle, not talking much but not feeling the silence either, and watch the dead leaves drifting down past the rocks in the cool-talking brook. The fire itself felt good, in spite of the sun, and it was good to hear the nervous twitter of the partridges in the apple trees just before it got too dark to pick out their heads along the sights of the gun. . . . Or is this like the day last spring we nodded at each other across the pool with the foam on it each time we held a broken-neck trout throbbing in the tight of our palms? Or the day we cursed the heat in the alder-circled meadow and our shirts stuck to our backs like broken blisters? The hay smelt good that night, just the same, and it was good to hear the wagon wheels groan on the sill just before the dark thunder-frown of the sky burst and the barn roof beat back the rain. I remember the night we ate our first supper in the house I had built with my own hands. That night the neighbours came in, and we danced half the night to the fiddles. It was easy with everyone, like with brothers, and we loved them all . . . and it was good that night to lie in bed and let sleep's drowsy wind blow out the candles of thought. The day they brought your brother Peter home loose in their arms before it was dinner time, his dead body so broken your mother could not hold it, that day was different. . . . And the next day. . . . And the next day. . . .

"Well what kind of a place suits *you*?" Martin said at last. David straightened.

"The city, of course! Who'd want to live in this God-forsaken hole when you can get a job in the city?"

"Did you say the *city*?"

"Yeah. The city," he said laconically.

Martin listened with sick wonder to this stranger who had been his son. The city. . . . It's *there* the days are the same. I thought it was very lonely in the city, the time I was there. The stone things move, but they do not change. My feet were always on stone. I could not walk on the ground and look over it and know it was my own. They never looked at the sky there, or listened for the rain.

When I looked at the sky there, the sun I saw was a strange one . . . it did not make friends with the stone. The stone houses were alike, and the days were alike, and never till they died could the people lie in bed at night and listen to rain on the corn after a long heat. They had nothing to breathe but their own tired breaths. I remember their faces. There was stone in them, too. They were all alike. They looked as if they never awoke from their tired dreams of the night. Their minds kept turning in their own tracks, like the weary wheels that could find no rest on the pavements. The soft-fingered women-faced men lived in houses, and the house-smell clung to everything they said or did when they went outside. When they talked, it was empty, because their eyes saw nothing but the stone things that their hands had not built . . . and none of them had anything to say that could not be said with words. It was very lonely there. They laughed too much. But not even love or death could melt their aloneness. Even when they laughed, their eyes did not change. And when they died, no one remembered, and there was nothing left of them.

I liked it in the city, now, this time, David thought. The street lights began to come on, a little before it was dark, and excitement seemed to stir in the busy pavements. The wind was not strong enough to lift itself above the street, but the women's skirts clung to their bodies as they passed. So many different women's bodies! What if they *didn't* speak? The bright, metallic faces of always-rich women seemed to shine in the shop-window light, and you knew you would feel clumsy and ashamed with them, but it was good to think of having their soft flesh alone somewhere in the dark. There was so much light there, then . . . and life. Like when you took off your work-clothes and shaved and felt smoother and brighter and ready for things. There was life, not death, at the end of the day. Here, my God . . . the same old bare maples weaving back and forth against a sky that made your lips blue just to look at it, and never the sound of a strange voice, and later the snow sifting lonely through the spokes of the wagon wheels. . . . What a God-forsaken place to be *young* in. Maybe his father didn't mind, they didn't seem to mind *missing* things when they got old. Old people didn't seem to dread being quiet and letting things slip like this. They thought it was because they were wise . . . it was because they were half-dead already. If he thought he'd ever get like that about things when he got old. . . . He'd never get old. He swore a desperate promise to himself that he'd never, never, never get that awful patience like his father . . . standing there now, with that stupid look on his face, like one of the oxen. . . .

"But Dave," Martin said slowly, "this place will be *yours* some day, you know that."

"What do *I* want of this old *place?*"

A whiteness came into Martin's face that was different from the whiteness of the cold or the weariness. He remembered the day his father had said the same thing to him. They had both felt shy and awkward, and he could say nothing, but as soon as he was alone, he had looked over this land, the tight tears of pride came warm into his eyes. He had kept this place, the best thing he had, till he could give it to his own son, and now when he offered it to David he saw it meant nothing. That he despised it. He had known through and through how his own father felt.

"It was always good enough here for *me*," Martin said.

"All right, but what did you ever *amount* to?"

Martin was stung into a sudden anger. "As much as *you* ever will, you. . . ."

Then he looked over the fields, slowly, and a break came into his anger. Why today, only a few hours ago, starting to plough, it had been, without a thought, so sweet, so safe, so sure . . . he and his son ploughing and him trying to show David how to turn the furrow better and David trying his best. Things just didn't come handy for David, it must be that. He had half felt Ellen working quiet and happy in the house and the smoke went straight from the chimney into the clear, sun-filled air and there had been no hurry or fret in the fields or the slow oxen or his thoughts. Now . . . it could never be the same again between him and David, now. Every time they said a sharp word to each other now, these sick things would all come back. . . . What if David was right? What *had* he ever amounted to? Well, he had been young here, and youth was very fresh and full here in the fields and the sun and very long, some of it never died, it grew green again with each April sun. He had had a wife of his own kind, and everything they had, they had got with their own hands, his hands and hers. There had been a lot of tiredness but there was always the quiet night afterwards and the slow kindly talk. There had never been an end of work, but you could always stop to talk across the fields to your neighbour, and you got along just the same. There had not been much money, but there had always been the sweet smell of bread in the kitchen and the soft song of wood in the kitchen stove. There had been no strangers among them, and when you died these men you had lived your whole life with would not work that day, even if there was clover to be hauled in and rain in the wind . . . and you would lie in the land that your hands and your feet knew best, and the same breezes you had breathed would always blow over you. Surely that was enough for a man. If your son. . . . If David. . . . It was hard to believe that your own son was not like you wanted him to be. But, Martin thought sadly, you couldn't make him see, if he didn't feel that way. You wished . . . but if he felt that way, there was no way to make him see.

"Well Dave," Martin said slowly, "if you're **bound** to go away, I suppose. . . ."

"Oh," David said impatiently, "let it go, let it go . . . I'll stay," he added sullenly.

He is almost afraid of me, Martin thought. He won't even talk it over with me. He has no use for my talk. He wants to keep me away from him. He don't think I can understand him at all. I try. . . .

He walked around to the oxen's heads and picked up the whip.

"Haw," he said quietly. "Just cut her light here, son."

David put his hands back on the handles but he didn't speak. He threw the plough around when they turned the furrows, so the chain jerked taut in the yoke. "Easy now, boys," Martin cajoled the oxen.

A bare little wind started in the bare maples. The sun burned cold and lonesome in the blind windows of the church across the road and the long withered grass bent over the cold grey sand in the middle of the built-up graves. Peter's grave. . . . Peter would coax to hold the whip. He could hardly make his small voice loud enough to stir the oxen, but they obeyed him. Martin could see the crazy nostrils of the running horses and then Peter's small crumpled body on the rock heap where the wheel had struck. . . .

The cows came up from the pasture, calling hollowly to be let in. The sky looked away from its own darkening face in the mud-bottomed puddles of the road. The blood in Martin's face came blue to the skin, and his blue eyes, a little faded with weariness, looked like frozen spots holding up the weight of his face. He walked back-to, guiding the oxen by the horns to help David keep the furrow straight, but David did not straighten his back, even when Martin stopped for a rock. Martin would come around and kick out the rock himself.

Martin blew on his hands and tried to start a smile in the corners of his tired, cold-thin, lips.

"Time for mittens, I guess. *Your* hands cold?"

"No," David said.

A shaft of the sun broke for a minute through the blue, wind-cold clouds. Long bands of it searchlit the grey rocks, without warming them.

"Snow comin'," Martin said.

The sun went down, and the sky made a few cold-pink patterns at the horizon. It would not be as sad again until April.

Martin turned the oxen for one more furrow. He could not stop, until he was *sure* how David. . . . Maybe if he kept on, David would say something himself about stopping, and he could show him then how ready he was to listen to him and take the oxen off the tongue.

"*I'll* never ask him to stop if he ploughs all night. . . ." David was so tired the muscles of his legs felt like a frayed rope and a tight cord drew his temples together. The blood seemed to drain from his face and throb heavy in his neck. The ashes of weariness sifted through the bright surface of his thoughts. The oxen lifted their heavy feet and deposited them carefully on the ground. The plough dug its slow way through the earth.

"I guess we're just gettin' her done in time," Martin said.

David said nothing.

"I guess this clears things up, about, for winter. You'll have a little more time to hunt, now, Dave."

Ellen came to the corner of the house, holding down her apron with one hand against the tug of the wind, and called supper.

"All right," Martin called back.

"Hungry, Dave?" he said.

"No."

Dave glanced at his father's face. For the first time he noticed how tired it looked. He felt sorry for his father, for a minute, and a little ashamed. He'd *have* to stay as long as his father was alive, he supposed.

They came to the end of the furrow. Martin hesitated.

"Well, I guess we'll let her go at that for tonight," he said. "We can wind her up in the morning, easy." He hesitated again.

"David," he said, "if you really *want* to go away. . . ."

David's impatience flared again. He forgot his father's face.

"Oh, for God's sake," he said, "can't you let that *drop*? I said I'd stay, didn't I? What more do you want? I'll stay here as long as *you're* here, anyway. So you need not worry."

So it is that way. A small coal touched suddenly against Martin's heart. He will wait, but he will be glad . . . so he can go away. If he was waiting for it, so the place would be all his own then, it would be . . . but he will be waiting, so he can go away. There will be a stranger here, and nothing will be done the same. There will be a strange name in my house, and maybe they will let the alders creep back over the acre field because they did not clear it for the first time and plough it with their own hands . . . and the grass will grow tall and strange over the graves.

He pulled the bolt from the tongue. It was true. It was true, then. He *had* no son. David took his hands from the plough. Martin waited for a minute to see if he would line the plough up for the next furrow in the morning. David did not move. Martin walked around to the plough. David went to the oxen's head, took up the whip and started with them to the barn. Martin pulled the plough around and lay the chain straight out along the next furrow. Ellen came to the corner of the house and called supper again, but Martin did not answer. He watched David take the oxen past the house. He saw Ellen say something to him, but David did not reply.

He bent down and dug the mud from the ploughshare. It shone underneath, where the earth had polished it, like a sword. The earth smelled cold and silent. He moved a few stones, absently, with his foot and stood for a minute with his eyes on the ground. Like the night they buried Peter. He felt lost in the long, dead day.

In the porch, he listened to see if David might be talking to the oxen. There was no sound but the bells, as David jerked the yoke-straps. Martin caught his breath quickly. He *had* no son. Peter was dead. He *had* no son, now. He scraped the dirt from his heels with a stick from the chipyard and went inside the house.

"Well, what in the *world* have you two been doing?" Ellen said, moving across the scrubbed soft-wood floor from the stove to the table. The warm breath of food rose sweet in the oil-lamplight. She held the dipper of water for Martin's hands over the basin in the sink. "Are you goin' to do a coupla more acres after supper?" she joked.

"Yeah, I was kinda thinkin' we might," Martin laughed.

But his laughter was heavy and grey, like a hawk rising.

CITY
AND COUNTRY

Another
Christmas

Christmas comes to the city too, in a way. . . . The air is clean and cold that day and in the streets the faces come alive and sometimes childlike, and people smile at strangers. This one day there is the strange warmth and excitement and kindness abroad, and when the dusk of Christmas Eve falls on the busy streets, for the first time the great green trees with all their artificial lights look happy. When the dark falls, the trees lighted behind the windows seem almost as kind as lamplights, and even the shopping crowds feel the strange stir in their hearts as if something incredibly thrilling were about to happen. . . .

Inside the apartment, Eve in her cool sure way had everything bright and in order. The other lights were carefully subordinated to the glimmer of the tree which stood in one corner with a few exotically wrapped packages of assorted sizes piled beneath it. The table glowed properly with simple crystal and silver and a single English holly centrepiece. The wine bottles each had a great bow of red ribbon. Eve herself with her easy silver way and luminous skin moved among the guests, listening, talking, and laughing with her pale bright laugh, like beads falling. They often wondered why Steve never wrote about women like his wife. He always wrote about the simple girls he had known as a child in the country.

This party Eve had arranged specially for him because it was an occasion. His first book was just out, and even the most chronically churlish reviewers had used no adjective smaller than "great". It ought to be the best Christmas Steve had ever had.

"Merry Christmas!" "Merry Christmas!" they were all shouting . . . the women with their quick eyes and nervous bodies and the men who could hold a glass in that casual way Steve had never quite mastered; and laughing with them, with the wine

29

lifting vaguely inside him, it felt like Christmas all right, the real thing, he thought. The bright things they said seemed very funny, with the wine, and he liked these people.

"My dear, you should *see* the strange package I found tucked away in Toby's closet. It must be for me and I'm simply frantic about it. It all goes up to a peak, but he *swears* it isn't a metronome. . . ."

"No thanks, Eve, I'm sticking to scotch tonight. The other seems to upset my metabolism or something. . . ."

"Good King Wenceslas . . . how about a chorus of Good King Wenceslas? . . . I like the part where it goes Stee-*eee*-ven. What do you know, it *is* the feast of Steven, isn't it! Eh, Steve?"

"We ran into Anne's on the way over and she had the most adorable little aspic . . . all reindeers and things, even to the antlers. . . ."

"That's damn good stuff, Steve. . . ."

"We should have Jackie here . . . he knows the most *salacious* little parody on 'The Night Before Christmas'. Have you heard Jackie. . . ."

"Why don't we call him? He'd be at Ginny's."

"But Ginny is *especially* dull on Christmas Eve, don't you think. . . ."

And of course in one corner, very seriously, over cigarettes:

"I suppose what Shaw really meant, if he meant anything at all. . . ."

"But really his *nudes* are appalling . . . they're all so sort of utilitarian, if you see what I mean. . . ."

"Why don't *we* attack for once, down through. . . ."

And then they were talking about Steve's book.

"It's uncanny, Steve, the way you seem to see right through people. It makes me definitely uneasy. . . ."

"Nice going, old man, *damn* nice going."

"That part about the little country girl . . . what's her name, Ellen or something? . . . that's *really* cute, Stevie. . . ."

Cute!

"But how do you keep from turning handsprings, Steve? To be able to write like that . . . good Lord, it must be so damned *wonderful*. . . ."

"Lucky beggar, you! Only having to work when you *feel* like it. . . ."

So it's wonderful to write, he thought. So it's such an easy job. Well, you don't know how white paper can be. You don't know what it is like in the ghost-world of words.

At first it had been a great new space to walk into and wonder, it was exciting to be another-time-and-space builder yourself, and you had a pity for the others with only one narrow life to live, their own, as it was. But then the real thing got less and less, because you were always watching it, it was only something to tell. And the first day you tried to tell a thing that had happened, truly, and the right-feeling words would not come, the ones that had a move and a speaking in them, the ones that brought the thing outside you, clearer and shapelier than you had ever thought you knew it . . . the first day those would not come at all but only the springless bones-of-words, and you sat there feeling the white-tight silence of the very doors and everyone else seemed to be busy with something alive, the real thing, and you thought surely in a little while, but you had to get up finally and leave it, you couldn't get your hands on it at all . . . they could not even *guess* what that sort of emptiness was like. And the other times when you did get something truly, then your mind was feverish and swarming with everything there was, to tell. If you walked in the woods then, there was the untold story in the way every single fir-tree was, to tantalize you, the small ones and the large ones and the straight ones and the one that leaned lonesome against the horizon all through the dark secret night . . . there were not only the big things then, the never-to-be-fathomed stuff of space and time, the human heart, the way the face is, the great gossamer-drifting mists of thought, but all the little things too . . . the pebble and the snail's eye and the sleepy cat-thoughts and the worm's track you never saw and the billionth blade of grass. There was more in any *one* of these little things than you could ever tell in your whole lifetime . . . there was more in the way the wagon-wheels stood there, lonely in the snow, that grey-blustery winter afternoon than you could even suggest. When you came out at dusk with your gun and stood there on the cold hill at the edge of the woods and there were the lonely wagon-wheels with the snow sifting through the spokes, and the dead apple-tree limbs, and you felt that nice lonely feeling about the whole world when it is dusk in the wintertime, and it was quiet, then, like death, when the dying is over and only the stillness is left . . . you couldn't tell that because there were a million things in it to tell,

31

and a million ways to tell every one of them, and only one way for each of them was right. And you tried desperately to find a single light that would come suddenly so that everything would fall into place as if you were looking at a picture that was only broken lines at first but as you looked at it, steadily, suddenly all the broken lines flowed into a single image, and the separate lines were gone and everything was part of the same thing.

But you never found that single light . . . that single plan. No one ever did. So how could the little separate part you had told matter at all?

And then they were all gone and he and Eve were alone.

"Shall we open them tonight?" Eve said.

"Why, yes, I think we might as well." He laughed. "I remembered one time when we were children we opened them on Christmas Eve, and then cried afterwards because we had not saved them for morning."

Eve's present for him was a brand new typewriter. She waited for him to exclaim.

"Don't you *like* it, darling?" she said.

"Of course!" he said. "It's a beauty. But really, Eve, the old one. . . ."

"But that one's *so* old, Stevie. You must have had it ever since you started."

It would be a little hard to explain to Eve, he thought, how he felt about the old typewriter.

The clock struck twelve.

"Merry Christmas!" Eve smiled at him.

"Merry Christmas, darling," he said softly, kissing her.

They were silent.

"What are you thinking about?" Eve said. "That's the trouble with you, Stevie, I never know what you're *thinking* about."

He was thinking about the Christmas he got the new skates.

He had gone with his father the afternoon before for the Christmas tree, and he had wondered how his father could be so calm. He knew *he* could never get calm about Christmas, no matter how old he got to be. The snow he prayed for had come and it lay smooth over everything except where the rabbits had made their odd snowshoe tracks across it, and it sparkled in the sun. Strange lips of it hung over the middle of the brook where he could still see the water running under holes in the shell ice. He made rabbit tracks of his own with the end of his mitten, the long-foot ones and the small dot with the thumb where both hind feet came down together. How good his father seemed. How good everyone he thought of seemed that afternoon. That night, when the lamp was lit and the fascinating smell of oranges was through the house and his mother busy with all sorts of mysterious things, he would sneak off now and then into the room where the tree was, and put his nose as close as he could to the little blisters of balsam and the places where the bark was skinned away to the glistening trunk beneath. The smell of the fir and the oranges was like a wine in his senses. Later, in bed, he could hear his mother and father laughing and making strange rustling noises behind the closed kitchen door, and he swam further and further and further off to sleep in an almost intolerably delicious excitement.

And there they were, next morning, the first thing he saw. Gleaming and clean like speed itself. And screwed right into the boots! That was the wonderful part. He was afraid they might be spring skates but these ones were screwed right onto the boots like the big boys' skates were.

He took them down to the meadow that afternoon all by himself. And *that* was the day . . . he could remember the very time it was in the afternoon, with the dark spruces just beginning to creep closer around the blue meadow-ice . . . that it came to him how to cross your skate over when you turned a corner. So you got the long clean sweep the bigger boys had when they were so sure of it they could do it faster, or slower, or clown it, or do it any way at all it was so sure with them. Once before on the old spring skates he'd almost got it, but the next time he tried, it was jerky, and after that if anyone was looking he wouldn't try to cross over at all, he'd just coast around and bend down to make out he was tightening his bootlace. But that afternoon . . . Lord, it was lovely that afternoon, he thought, with the new skates and half-remembering all the time that the Christmas tree and the oranges would still be there when he got home . . . that time he had done it and he didn't know, in his head, just how, but he knew it was *right*, that now his legs knew it, to repeat it, whenever they liked. Now he was sure of it. And that first time you crossed over on the new skates and felt the cool wing-sure dip of it and knew that now you had it, really had it. . . .

"What *are* you thinking about, Steve?" Eve said.

33

"I was just thinking about one Christmas I got new skates."

"And," Eve laughed, "I suppose you're going to tell me that pair of skates made Christmas more fun than a best-seller! Stevie darling, you're getting sentimental in your old age."

"It's just possible," he said.

You Could Go
Anywhere Now

Mrs. Andrews held the parlour curtain back frankly when they passed the house without stopping, but she couldn't see either of their faces, David's or his wife's, for the little whirlwind of dust that spun behind the car down the hot summer road. A dull flash of hurt burned in her own face. David, who had been like her own son, would be like the others now.

The others were never quite the same when they came back from the city. There was always that little defensiveness you couldn't help feeling with them. Even the special clothes they had for everything they helped with on the farm—the big coloured hats of the women and the white pants of the men, just soiled enough—seemed to make an awkwardness between them.

It was worse still with the ones that came with them, the real city ones. Their kind of friendliness made you feel foolish somehow. The funny eagerness of the women especially, as if the questions they kept asking about things in the country that were plain enough to anybody would please you right through. As if you wouldn't know it was just bad manners to act like that.

David's wife, she thought, is one of those.

She would have that sure look they all had in their faces, coming into the house to call on her. Picking up a shell or something off the mantle and saying, oh look, isn't that *darling*? As if it must flatter you all over to have your little keepsake amuse her. As if you didn't know she wouldn't think of acting that way in anyone's house in the city. Coming right around mealtime maybe and catching her before she'd changed her dress, but never thinking that would matter. Never thinking that a country woman would mind meeting another woman for the first time when she didn't look her best or have her good dishes on the table, or that she should give her own appearance a thought. Never thinking that a country woman was a woman in the same sort of way she was at all.

She would spoil David, too. The men became like their wives when they married the city ones. A sudden anger tightened in Mrs. Andrews's kind ready face.

Because David had never been like the others when he came back before. He worked in the same old clothes he had always worked in. And when he came into your house it was the same old way, quietly but at home, with no need to talk if there was nothing that needed talking about. He had come into her house now she was alone and lonely the same way he used to come in when he was a child and she had kept him those three wonderful years after his mother died, more tenderly than like a son because she had never had a son of her own.

David had seemed to belong to all of them here that way. There had never been any jealousy of David, even after he had gone so far beyond them that the city ones knew his name now too. It was as if one of your own family had *shown* the city ones.

That's why the thought kept circling in her mind, if there could only be some mistake—if there was only some way it could be Anna after all in the car with him today. Anna was a girl from home, and that would be the surest way of keeping him always among them. He had planned to marry Anna when they left this place together, and no one had ever dreamed that he would change his mind, because David would want a wife who had no strangeness with his own people.

Until the word came suddenly, not two weeks ago, that it was all over between David and Anna. That he was going to marry one of the city ones. It was as if the son you were surest and proudest of had gone over to the other side.

"Well—?" David said to his wife, silent beside him on the seat of the car.

"Do I have to say something?" she said, smiling.

"No," he said, "there was never any watching. That was the thing, right from the first."

He drove on slowly, letting the fullness of the minutes take that strange song in him, because he and she and this place could all talk to each other or be quiet together in the same way.

"Home—" she said softly, and she put one hand on his sleeve just tightly enough to feel the flesh beneath it. But she did not do it with any trickery, conscious that the light way was the right way. "Coming home with you, David—"

"It's home for you too, isn't it?" he said. "That's the nice part. After a while a man can't go home alone. You can't do anything alone, really. The unit is two people."

That was the thing about the other one. The one who had so *nearly* been with him in the car now. The one with only the bright city thoughts. This place today would mean nothing to that one—the way of it when the green mist of growing hung everywhere in the spring air, or later when the paler green of the long fields shimmered in the silence of the noon sun after the hay was cut and the little sadness of Fall was first quiet in the dark mountains, or later still when the Christmas kindliness was all through the living green of the white-shouldered spruces. Driving along with him today, it would have been as if she were leafing over an album of views, idly. None of the voice of this place would have come through to her, and he and she would have had to talk.

It had been so nearly too late when he found out that she despised him a little too. Because he could never leave this place. Because it would always be home to him. No matter what he did or where, the good slowness of earth and the little loneliness of it that was a man's best company, things like that, would always be in him as they were in the people who still lived here.

But with her he'd have had to keep that part of his heart secretly, and go to it alone. And you can't do it that way, if it's any good between you and your wife. You have to go all the important places in the heart together.

You could go home with this one beside him now, he thought. This one knew the light way, but because she had the quiet part too, because she could hear the same voice he heard in these places he had been young in, you could always go home now no matter where you were, just to speak of it to this one. You could go *anywhere* with this one now, or do anything, just to speak of it or think of it together, and there was no hunger in anything anymore.

"Dave," she said, "did you really understand about Mrs. Andrews?"

"Sure," he said quickly, because this was the first thing he hadn't quite understood with her. "This evening will be just as good anyway. It was just that I always *did* stop for a minute on the way by."

"I know," she said. She glanced at herself quickly in the car mirror. "But, Dave, can't you *see* what a sight I am? Look at my hair."

"You look fine," he said. "It wouldn't make any difference to Mrs. Andrews how you looked."

"Which is it, darling," she said, laughing, "do I look fine or doesn't it make any difference?"

"You look wonderful," he said.

"No, but really," she said, "I'd like to look nice. You *don't* understand . . . a little. You think it's some sort of vanity. But I'm your bride, Dave, and I'd just like to look nice for someone I think so much of and who thinks so much of you. I think I *ought* to fix myself up for Mrs. Andrews. Don't you see?"

"Okay," he said, seeing it her way now. "Come to think of it, tonight is better. I want to get her something. I always brought her something from the city, but I guess I had you too much on my mind this time."

"We *should* have brought her something, Dave," she said. "Something real nice." She thought a minute. "I wonder," she said, "would there be anything of mine. . . ."

"Stationery?" he said.

"Dave!" she said, grimacing and striking his shoulder a little blow. "Not *stationery*!"

"Well then. . . ?" he said.

"Dave," she said, "would you think it wasn't the nicest thing you ever gave me if I parted with that precious little bottle of Chanel?"

He stared at her, half-incredulous. "Why, no," he said. "But for Mrs. Andrews? What in the world would a country woman do with a bottle of fussy *perfume*?"

"What do you think, silly?" she said. "Water the geraniums? You don't think a country woman likes things like that less than any other woman, do you? A little bit of really *nice* perfume for special occasions, she'd love it."

"She might, at that," he said slowly. "I guess I wouldn't know."

And the other one wouldn't either, David thought.

It was only last Christmas he'd spoken to her about something for Mrs. Andrews. "Don't ask *me* what to send her darling," she'd said. "A bungalow apron, I suppose. I can't think of anything else a woman could use back in *that* place."

Anna had been born in this place, he thought, but she had never really known it at all. But Katharine, the city one, who had never seen these people before, was coming home more even than he.

EBB
AND FLOW

The Quarrel

Do you know what quarrelling is like between a man and a woman to whom the language of quarrelling is an alien tongue?

When you go outside from the kitchen afterward, if you are the man, the leaves wave absently in the movement of the August air that is more heat than breeze; and everything you work with, the fork or the scythe or the handle of the plough, sags, heavy to the touch. Your thoughts stumble inside your head, and time comes inside and hurts there. You think it must be noon a dozen times, but scarcely an hour has passed.

If you are the woman, you reach into the corners of the zinc beneath the stove legs as carefully as ever with the broom, and stoop as carefully as ever to pick up the twist of white thread embedded in the raised roses of the hooked rug, but the rug doesn't seem like anything your own hands ever made. You were going to have a change for dinner, but it's too late now; there is a cast of irrevocable lateness about everything. You catch a glimpse of your face in the mirror over the sink, and it seems as if the mirror must be lying, to show it enclosed and with shape. You press the tip of the flatiron into the fancy points of rickrack braid on the apron, but you don't feel the inner smile that was always there at a thing that was extra trouble to be made pretty.

The kitchen and the fields go dead, with a kind of singing remoteness. And when the hum of the anger has died completely away, there is nothing left—nothing but that curious drawing between you, as if you were tied together with an invisible cord on which all the minutes were strung to intolerable heaviness, but never to actual breaking.

I didn't know that all this was happening between mother and father that Saturday morning, of course, because I was only ten. But I knew the day was spoiled. And the next day. I knew what Sunday would be like.

It wouldn't be the perfect August Sunday, the first Sunday after the hay was cut, with the nice hiatus about it as if even the fields knew it was a day of rest, and the tail ends of all the jobs that weren't quite finished lacking the insistence they seemed to have on a weekday. My father would not drowse on the kitchen lounge in the long restoring forenoon, while mother wandered with that special Sunday leisure through her flower garden, pulling a weed here and there, stooping to hold a bright poppy in her hand like a jewel, bringing a dipper of water from the well and holding apart the spicy leaves of the geranium so the roots got all of it, and tiptoeing in past him with a bouquet of the splashy nasturtiums for each of the lamp rests on the organ.

And after dinner, father would not change into the striped drill pants with the size tag still on the waistband and his fine shirt and his fine shoes. Mother would not go upstairs and come down adjusting the wonderfully intricate coral brooch at the neck of her dress. And I wouldn't wait with the thrill of a minor conspiracy, though it was a simple thing, to walk together with them to the garden.

The hay was cut, but we wouldn't walk to the garden with that funny feel of freedom, because, though we could still see the darker-green line of the crooked path we had used through the stringy grass, now our feet could go anywhere they liked. Nor through the garden, where it lay exposed at last to the full kiss of the sun; looking for any cast of ripening in the tomatoes, parting the secrecy of the cucumber vines to see if any fruit lay on the ground beneath, gauging the number of days before the corn would be really yellow, or calling a greeting, smiling though our faces couldn't be clearly seen that far, to a neighbour strolling through his garden the same way.

Father would not change his clothes at all tomorrow. As soon as he had milked and fed the pigs, he would fill his tobacco pouch and get a handful of matches from the canister behind the pantry door and go outside, without asking mother what time she planned to have dinner. She might be doing the chamber work or putting clean newspapers under the rows of preserves down cellar, but she seemed to feel the instant he left the house and I would see her come to the dining-room window and watch, in that curious secret way, to see whether he went to the wood lot or the back meadows.

The whole kitchen would seem to catch its breath when his step sounded on the porch again, exactly at noon. As we ate silently, mother would seem to know, without watching, the minute he was ready for his tea; but she'd set it down where he could reach it, she wouldn't pass it to him. And if they both put a hand out for the sugar bowl at the same time, something so tight and awful would strain across the table that I'd feel like screeching.

Right after dinner, father would leave again. Mother would dress up a *little*—I don't think, if she were dying, she could have sat through Sunday afternoon in a housedress—but she wouldn't go outside. She'd be quiet with the catalogue for a bit, but just when I'd think her mind was taken up, she'd drop the catalogue and begin that awful wandering from room to room. As if each familiar thing promised her absorption and then failed her.

When I'd hear her swivelling up the organ stool, her intake of breath, caught before it became a real sigh, and then the first pitifully inaccurate chords of "Abide With Me," I'd rush outside, myself.

And no matter how late I played, or with whom, or at what fascinating game, or no matter how angry I got with myself that I couldn't be insensitive to my parents' quarrels as other kids were, I'd get that awful feeling in the pit of my stomach when I came near the house again that evening. Then we would sit silently, but each moving when another moved, with the Sunday hiatus stifling as a thunder pocket now.

I'd go to bed early, to escape it. But it was no use. I'd listen for the movement of mother taking the clock from the mantelpiece, and start when I heard it. I could see father then, sitting there in the loud-silent kitchen with even the tick of the clock gone, staring at the floor a minute after he had taken off his boots, before he followed her. I would hear the softer than usual pad of his woollen socks on the stairs and then there would be nothing. The very boards of the old house would seem to sing with that listening stillness.

That's exactly how it turned out to be. I have no trouble to *remember* the particular torture of that day.

You see, that was the August Sunday which was to have been twice as wonderful as ever before because it had in it the looking ahead to a tomorrow more wonderful than any day I had ever known. Monday was the day that we, and we alone from all the village, were going to the Exhibition in Annapolis.

I had never been to the Exhibition before. There was to be a travelling show. (I had studied the poster so long I knew the face of Madame Zelda as well as my own, she who would tell my fortune though she didn't even know I existed.) There was to be a merry-go-round. ("Mother, do they really go as fast as an automobile?") There was to be the excitement of so many strange faces. There was to be ice cream. And those were the days when ice cream was something that made a high priest of the man who scooped it with such incredible nonchalance out of the deep freezer, and it didn't seem as if the ten cents you laid on the counter could possibly pay for it.

I should have had warning of the quarrel. The moments before it had been so perfect.

We had been wrapping the tablecloth of tiny, tiny, intricately mortised blocks, that mother was to enter in the fancywork class. She kept folding it, this way and that, trying to find a way it would not muss; even father hung about the table, wanting to be in on the thing; and I stood there, tingling with willingness to hold my finger on exactly the right place while mother tied the second knots.

She had made a great show of pretending that she'd never have dreamed of sending it in if the others hadn't kept at her, and we never mentioned the possibility of its winning a prize. But in our hearts, none of us had any doubt whatever that it would be the most beautiful thing there and would get first place.

When I took it out to the mailbox, the laborious lettering on the wrapper completed at last, there was that wonderfully *light* feeling in all of us. The moment was so perfect that even the consciousness of its perfection sprang into my mind.

Always before, when this had happened, I had thought of something sad at once, as a sort of protection. If only, I castigated myself afterward, I had not neglected to do that this time. . . .

It doesn't matter how this quarrel started. The thing is, their quarrels always ended the same way. Actually, what happened, my father began poking about in the bottom of the dish closet where mother kept the wrapping paper.

"Did you see that sheet of paper with the lumber tally on it?" he said.

"What did it look like?" mother said.

"It was just a sheet of paper with some figures on it," he said.

"Where did you put it?" she said.

"I put it in here," he said. "It ain't here now."

"Let me look," she said. She went through exactly the same papers he had, but she didn't find it.

"It ain't there," father said, with the first hint of annoyance. "I ought to know it when I see it."

Mother looked through all the papers again.

"You didn't burn it with them scraps from the package, did you?" father said.

"No," mother said, "of course not. I never burn anything that's any good." But she went and looked in the stove just the same. There was nothing but ashes there now.

"Well, what did you stick it *in* there for?" she said suddenly.

"I'd like to know where I'd put anything that—" father said. "You're always burnin' somethin'!"

"*Ohhhhhh*—" mother said. She sighed. "I wish I'd never bothered with that tablecloth."

"*Ohhhhhh*—" father said. He started to pace about the kitchen, the way he always did when he was angry. The cat brushed against his legs and he stepped on her tail. Her screech startled him so he gave her a kick with his foot. "*Git* out from under my feet," he said. Mother put the cat outdoors, without saying a word; as if he were a man who was cruel to animals and she couldn't bear to watch it.

"Now I'll have to count that lumber all over again," father said.

"Oh," mother said, "you'd think that was going to kill you—"

I ran out of the house then, because I knew what the rest of it would be like. Now they were both angry beyond embarrassment or caution at their quarrelling; whenever they could think of nothing else to say, they'd say something false and cruel. "Oh, no, no one ever gets tired but *you*—" "Well, what do you think it's like for *me*?" "I got feelings, too—"

I ran around in circles outdoors, the whole day burst and tumbling about me. They had broken it, like glass, and no matter how perfectly you fitted the pieces together again, you'd know that the mending was there. I was such a foolish child that when a thing which was to have been perfect was spoiled the least bit, it was spoiled entirely. If I as much as scratched the paint on my new wagon I wanted to take the axe and smash the whole thing to bits.

I hated them both then, equally. I'd never speak to them again as long as I lived—I'd run away to town—I'd die. . . .

We were all up Monday morning before dawn. But it wasn't like other mornings when we'd eaten in the magic minutes of lamp-light, preparing to go somewhere special. That awful speechless synchronization of movement between mother and father still went on. She was taking the strainer off the clothesline exactly when he set the milk pails beside the scalded creamer. His blue serge suit was laid out on the bed just before he went up to dress; and just as he was walking back through the hallway to the kitchen again, she was on *her* way, through the dining room, to dress, herself.

I hated them separately, then. First one and then the other. When father took every cent of his money from the tureen in the dish closet and then came back and asked me (because mother hadn't offered) to brush off the back of his coat, I hated mother. "Father, why don't you get someone to *help* you mow that old back meadow next week?" I said, loud, so she could hear. When mother came downstairs and took the precious little bottle of perfume from behind the pendulum of the dining-room clock, her face with the same tight look on it that his had, I hated father. "Let *me* take that creamer down cellar," I said. "It's too heavy for you."

There is something about changing one's clothes and the prospect of movement that stales the validity of an old quarrel. I think either of them might have spoken then. But I suppose that whenever father was tempted to speak the watchful drop of acid would touch a spot where his pride was still raw: "The time I set the boiling kettle on the new oilcloth, I said I was sorry, but she made out I did it on purpose just the same—She says *she* has a hard life." And when mother was tempted to speak, the same whisper would stir up the whole wind of forgotten hurts: "The time I scrubbed till I thought my back would break and then he tracked right through the house with his muddy boots on, just because he couldn't keep Tom *Hannon* waiting a minute for that pair of traces in the attic—He says *he* has a hard life." And when they'd let the minute pass, the silence itself had a kind of un-shakable fascination.

We had a sixteen-mile drive before us. It was one of those glorious mornings you get sometimes in late August, with a cleanness about it more of spring than of early fall. Little hair nets of dew clung here and there on the glistening grass. The waking call of the birds sounded sharp and new. It would be hot later, very hot, but now it was cool. Dark shadows of the alders fell across the dusty road, cool as shadows inside a well.

We didn't keep saying what a perfect day it was for the Exhibition, though. No one spoke at all. I didn't ask questions about any of the things that had happened in any of the places we passed, waiting with more, rather than less, excitement, because I already knew the answers from so many stories before. It was all right when the horse was jogging. But when he slowed down to a walk, with the spinning of the wheels a sound of scraping only, as if we were bound to the road, the stretches from turn to turn looked endlessly long. The only way I could sit still at all was to pretend that, with hard enough thinking of the town, some elastic tension would draw us suddenly from here to there.

This was the day that was to have been the most wonderful in my whole life. . . .

I suppose the moment when we turned the corner by the old block-house and first came in sight of the Exhibition itself was most like the moment when the forces of the ingoing and the outgoing tide balance exactly. I think it was then that the quarrel lost all its *colour*, like the flame of a lamp that has burned on into the daylight. There suddenly was the high board fence that encircled the actual wonder and all the throng. We became different people.

We seemed to shrink a little, somehow. Each of us could see, helplessly, as if noticing it was a kind of betrayal, that our clothes were Sunday clothes that had stiffened in the midst of the townspeople who had no idea that they were dressed up.

I think mother must have longed to straighten father's tie, and I couldn't help wishing he would put his coat on again, to cover up the sweat marks that edged the straps of his braces. I wished that mother would take off the sprig of fern she had pinned on her coat lapel, so wilted now that the safety pin showed through. I wiped the dust off the shiny round toes of my brown shoes and for the first time I wished they weren't so patently new. I took off the red-banded straw hat I had spent so long tilting at the right angle, and thrust it beneath the tasselled sewing-machine throw that mother had brought along to protect our good clothes.

Mother and I waited at the gate while father put out the horse. I forgot almost everything else then but the excitement to come. I watched the throng of people going in and the trickle of people coming out. It seemed incredible that there was no change of any kind in their faces the instant they stepped from the inside to the outside. How *could* they not look back, in soberness, or in satiety, or in longing? How could they *bear* to leave while it was still going on?

When father joined us again, silent still, and with that subtle little flicker of adjustment in mother when she saw his approach, we moved toward the ticket window. Just before we got there, he said to her, "Do you want any money?"

I don't know what there was about that question. It was a curiously hurting thing, to have to ask, and to hear. No matter what had happened, the thought of her maybe having not enough *money*, on a day of pleasure—

"I got money," she said.

At last we were inside. I wish I could say that I stayed close with them all that day. But I deserted them almost at once. They moved through the clotted crowd so slowly. The stream of townspeople kept dividing us and father would step aside to let them pass. I wished he would walk straight ahead and let them move aside of *him*. I was suddenly angry with them because they didn't talk and laugh together as the others did. I left them, though father had given me a bright fifty-cent piece, so much more wonderful than if it had been in small coins, and mother had given me a quarter though I could see there were no bills in her purse at all. I left them because I thought the only way I could savour the wonder utterly was to know it alone.

It's an odd truth that when a child who has played too much alone pictures himself in the scene of a carnival occasion, he is invariably at the hub of its spirit; but when the time actually comes, he finds himself at the farthest point of its periphery. It was like that then.

Not that some of it could have been more wonderful. The ice cream. The ecstasy of the merry-go-round, heightened by the very dread of the horses beginning to slow down. The songs of the cowboys. It was not they, it was *I* who was singing. But in between the moments when the movement or the magic swung me irresistibly out of my own body, the sea of strange faces was like a kind of banishment. I stood there among them with such a feeling of nakedness that I wondered why they didn't seem to notice it.

When I came to the howdahlike booth of Madame Zelda, the sense of my fortune being a thing between just the two of us was gone altogether. The others crowded so close and surely everything she said could be heard. I stood there with my quarter tight and ready in my palm, but no matter how often I struck myself cold inside with the certain resolution to speak to her after she was through with that very next person, when my chance came my heart would beat so hotly that I simply couldn't get a word out. An agony of heat and cold alternated inside me until she put her jewelled hands flat on the counter, leaned out, and called. "Have your future prophec*iiiiii*ed-a." It seemed she was staring directly into my face. I made a frantic pretence of looking for something I had lost on the ground and moved quickly away.

I joined my mother and father again.

We came to the machine that registers your strength by the height a ball shoots upward at the blow of a hammer.

"Try it," I whispered to father. The man before him, a tall man with thin white town arms, had sent it up two thirds of the way. I wanted father to show them he could send it right to the top.

Father swung the hammer and the ball shot up almost as far as it had gone before, but not quite, and then fell back. "I guess I need more beans for that," he said, half-addressing the men about us. They glanced at him, without smiling, as if they didn't understand what he meant, or as if his futile little joke was out of place. He stepped back, his own tentative smile twitching and drying up on his face.

And it was just after that that a man and a woman went by on mother's side, and we couldn't help hearing the woman whisper to her husband, "Did you get the perfume? I wonder if she took a bath in it. What is it, Cauliflower Blossom?"

The day was very hot now, and our legs were tired. We walked on past the lunch counter where scraps of bitten food lay on the ground with the dust adhering to them, and past the booth where the sweating men waited for a dead-eyed attendant to set up the Kewpie dolls.

"Are you goin' to take the tablecloth home with you?" father said.

"I might as well," mother said.

Father walked ahead, inside the building, to the central bench where the prize-winning objects were displayed, but it wasn't there. Our hearts skipped in dismay. Had it arrived too late? Had it been lost in the mail?

The tablecloth was there all right, but not on that bench. It was back in one corner, half-concealed by a hooked rug. It hadn't won any prize at all. And now all of us could see why. It was *not* as beautiful as the other things. We couldn't help seeing now that the pattern we had thought so involved was really plain alongside the peacocks in the prize-winning centrepiece, and that the texture of its material lacked altogether the light spiderweb delicacy of the other's crochet.

I couldn't stand the silence then. I slipped away, hardly able to keep from running before I got outside.

I ran so fast down the steps when I did get outside that I collided head on with a boy from town. We both tumbled. I picked myself up and half-smiled at him.

"Do you want to fight?" he said, coming close and puffing out his body.

"N-no," I said.

"Well, then, watch where you're going," he said.

When mother and father came out of the building, mother with the tablecloth wrapped up under her arm, I said, "Let's go home."

Mother looked at father. "I'm ready whenever you're ready," she said.

He said, "I'm ready to go whenever you are."

We must have been halfway to the gate before I remembered Madame Zelda. I *couldn't* leave without that. "You go on—" I said.

I ran back toward Madame Zelda's booth without any explanation. The customers had thinned out now. She was sitting sidewise, with her chin cupped in one hand, talking to the man who ran the merry-go-round. I was so close I could hear what she was saying. She said, "If I have to set here and dish out much more o' this tripe in this bloody heat, I'm gonna murder the next one that comes along." I was so close I could see the green mark that the bright ring she was twirling on one finger had left on her hand beneath.

I turned. I couldn't see father and mother anywhere. And then I started to run again. I think if I hadn't caught up with them before they reached the gate, if they had left me in there alone, I'd have burst out crying.

Now here is where I wish for the subtlety to show you, by the light of some single penetrating phrase, how it was driving home. But I can only hope that you will know how it was, from some experience of your own that was sometime a little like it.

Do you know how my father felt, remembering the woman laughing at the perfume mother had thought such a touch of splendour, and thinking of the time he'd known she wanted to go to the magic lantern show in the schoolhouse because she changed her dress right after supper, in case he should offer to take her, but he'd been angry from chasing cows and said nothing, and she'd taken off her good dress again, saying nothing either, because she knew he was tired? Do you know how he felt, remembering the clothes of the town women that he could never afford to buy her the likes of, and thinking how he'd told her she should have *some* men, they'd show her?

Do you know how my mother felt, remembering his face when the town men had made him appear weak and silly about the strength machine, and thinking of the time she'd gone to the cabbage supper alone, giving him to think he was only pretending to be tired, and coming home to see the single plate and the cup without a saucer where he'd got his own supper on the pantry shelf? Do you know how she felt, remembering him spending all his money on us today as if it were not the price of a bag of flour, and thinking how she'd told him that if he had *some* women they'd put him in his boots?

Do you know how I felt, remembering I had wished that father would put his coat on, and thinking of the Christmas when there was hardly money for bread, but when there had been a sled and crayons for me just the same?

Do you?

Perhaps then you will understand why a different kind of silence had mounted all day, sorer still, after the shifting of the tide. Perhaps you will understand what it was like driving along that night, thinking about the tablecloth, but being able to say nothing more to mother than "Let me take that basket over here, out of your way," or "Are you *sure* you got lots of room?"

And perhaps you will see how a point of fusion might be found after all. In the moment after the cat had brushed our legs in an ecstasy of welcome home, and the faithful fields had been found waiting for us, unaltered . . . after we had changed our clothes, father flipping the straps of his overalls so easily over each shoulder; mother tying behind her, without looking, the strings of the apron that seemed to be the very personification of suppertime; and me feeling the touch of the ground on my feet as immediate as the touch of it on hands, when I took off my stiff shoes and went, in my sneakers, for the kindling. Then it was that mother unwrapped the tablecloth and put it on the dining-room table again.

"It's the prettiest thing I ever seen," father said, "I don't care—"

That was the moment of release. Everything of the quarrel vanished then, magically, instantly, like the stiffness of a sponge dipped suddenly in water.

Because he spoke no less truly than with penitence. The tablecloth *was* more beautiful than anything else now—*here*, where it belonged.

I think I saw then how it was with all of us. Not by understanding, of course, but, as a child does sometimes, with the lustrous information of feeling. My father could lift a bale of hay no man at the Exhibition could budge, but there was a knack in a thing like the strength machine he was helpless against. It hadn't been humbleness that made him step aside for the town men to pass, any more than it had been fear that made me retreat from the town boy who wanted to fight. My mother's hat was as lovely as ever, now it was back in the bag in our closet. This sureness when we were home couldn't be transplanted; but that's why, when we had it all about us and in us, like an invisible armour, it was such a crying thing to hurt each *other*.

Bright pictures of the things I had seen that day still echoed like heat lightning in my mind. But they were two-dimensional. Mother coming to the corner of the shop as if she knew just when our feet were beginning to stumble, and telling father to make that the last furrow, she was having dinner a little early—Father edging the borders of the flower garden so perfectly by just his eye, while mother and I stood by with such strange closeness, because this wasn't *his* work at all—Watching the cows race to the tub after a day on the sun-baked marsh, to fill their long throats ecstatically with the cool well water—These things only were real.

I listened to father and mother talking in the kitchen that night, after I had gone to bed. I listened to them coming up the stairs together. I heard father take the change from his pocket and lay it on the bureau. I heard the murmur of their voices, low in the room, like the soft delicious drum of sleep in my ears. I thought of the quarter that had been so miraculously saved from squandering on my fortune—I could buy father a staple puller and mother a mixing spoon with it, for Christmas. I had never been so consciously happy in my whole life.

But I didn't take any chances this time. I repeated the words from my prayer, quickly, intensely, "If I should die before I wake. . . . If I should die before I wake. . . ."

I awoke and I heard mother and father talking in the kitchen. I thought, the hay is cut, the hay is cut . . . and this morning we will all walk together through the garden. I could feel already the exaltation when I chose the largest stalk and, as they watched, pulled the first new potatoes from the sweet crumbling earth.

The Clumsy One

Did you ever strike your brother? I don't mean with a blow. Sometimes when we were children and a flash of child's anger would make a sudden blindness in my brain, I'd strike David any place my blind hands came to. I don't care about those times. He'd never strike me back; but afterward I would ask to borrow his jackknife or something. He'd know I didn't really want it to use. He'd know that when I said "thanks, Dave," the words were really for my contrition.

I didn't do it with a blow that day.

I was standing right where I'm standing now, the day I struck David. I still stand, with my hoe idle, and remember it, whenever I come to this spot in the row. It was just such a summer's day as this, with the bowing heat of the sun turning the petals of the daisies inward and wilting the leaves of the apple trees in immobile patience for the night dew. Little watermarks of heat rose from the asphalt road where the cars passed back and forth beyond the sidehill.

If David had been alongside me, it might not have happened. But they got out of the car and came across the field quietly, to surprise me. I didn't know they were there until their voices made me start. David was at the bottom of another row, and before he came opposite us again I had time to plan it.

That was my first summer home from college. David didn't go to college, though he was the older. There was only money enough to send one of us, and there had never been any question which of us it would be. Because even as children it was I who was clumsy with anything outside the shadow world of books, and it was David who had the magic sleight for anything that could be manoeuvred with his hands. I don't know why the quick, nervous way of my mind seemed to make me the special one of the family. I could see instantly the whole route of thought that led to the proof of a geometry theorem, without having to feel it out step by step. But surely that was a poorer talent than to have the sure touch of David's fingers on the plough handles, that could turn the long shaving of greensward from one end of the field to the other without a single break.

I remember the first day *I* tried to plough. The sod would ribbon back cleanly for a bit; and then just when it seemed easy, I'd move the handles too much one way or the other, because I was thinking about it, and suddenly the whole strip of sod would flop back into the row in one long undulation. As it happened again and again, a hairspring of anger kept tightening inside me. I stopped once and tried to catch the sod with my hands; but the earth split where my hands were trying to hold it and the tail of the sod went slipping back behind me.

"You're trying to plough too deep, Dan," David said.

The hairspring broke. "Oh, is that so!" I shouted. "Well, do it yourself then, if you're so smart."

I turned to leave the field. When I was in a temper, the blot of anger seemed to strike all light and breath out of the place I was standing, like a blow in the stomach.

"Danny! For God's *sake* . . ." David said. Not angrily, but patiently. Because, for all his own quiet mind, he understood me so well he knew there was no sting of meaning in the words I couldn't stop.

I don't care about that time. The anger was over as soon as David spoke. I put my hands back on the plough handles. When we got to the top of the row, I looked back and said, "Now that's a pretty job, what?" and we both laughed. And then I asked him, the way the asking of help from another can be such a warming thing when anger between you has just passed, "What do I *do*, Dave—do I hold them too much this way or *that* way?"

He said, "You're ploughing a little too deep, Danny, that's all."

I let him show me then. And the next time down the furrow I tried terribly hard to keep the sod from breaking, to show David how earnestly I was trying to learn from him—

I went to college and David didn't, but I don't care about that. Maybe I always had the best of things, but it wasn't that I took them from the rest of the family, selfishly. It wasn't as if there was ever any dividing among us; our needs were met out of what we all had together, as each required. There was a sort of shy pride and a fierce shielding of me, because I was the one in the family who was weak in the flesh, but had the quick way with learning. One Christmas I got a set of books with real leather binding, while David got only a sled. But I knew that as they watched my face glow just to touch those books, the pride and wonder of knowing that one of their own family could feel a thing like that, was a better share in the books than my own possession.

It was I who got two suits the year I went to college, and David none; because I must look as good as the strangers I went among. But I don't care about that. If it had been David going away, I'd have given up my suit just as gladly. The thought that someone in the train might have the *chance* to laugh at his clothes, even though he bore their laughter quietly and without protest, would have made such a fierce hurt for him in me that I'd have given up anything I had to make his appearance equal to theirs.

I don't care about those things. But they were the things I thought about that day I struck him, just the same. I felt the shame of my action that day heavy in me, even before the others had gone; but I couldn't seem to help what I did. Sometimes there is a cruel persuasion you can't resist in the hurting of the one who understands you best, even as it hurts you more.

You see, the people who surprised me that day were some of the ones I had known at college.

I had just quarrelled with David about the distance between the potato hills. I told him he'd dropped the seed too close. He said there was no sense in wasting space. It was no more than a discussion, to him, until I shouted, "Yes, yes, yes, you're so stubborn—"

I wasn't really shouting at David. It was only the rankling at my own helplessness to hoe more than one row to his three, or to capture the knack he had of cutting the weeds and loosening the earth between the hills in a single stroke, just grazing the stalks of the plants themselves, that was speaking. The tremble of anger was still obliterating my attention when they sneaked up behind me. I never heard a sound of them until they spoke while my back was still turned.

"D'ya suppose he knows what he's doing?" Steve said.

I turned, startled. "Steve! Perry! Well. . . ."

"We're taking the census," Perry said, in mock seriousness. "Is your name Daniel Redmond? What was your income last year? Can you read?"

"Come on," I laughed. "Come off it."

They had the smooth city way of talking, with a bit of laughter or a glib word always ready to bridge the small pauses; the way of not having to make the meaning that ran along in their minds match the sound track at all. David's straight talk, with the silences in it a way of speech too, would have seemed stupid to them.

I didn't call David to the side of the field by the fence. And when he heard us, hoeing over in the potato rows, I talked their way too—for him to hear. David had never heard me talk like that before. I let him think that was my *real* way of talking. The way I talked when I was with my own kind. A way he could never talk to me at all.

"How's Smokey?" I was saying. "And Chuck? What's Bill Walton doing this summer? It's funny, I was just wondering this minute if Bill had ever patched up his rift with Eleanor." (That was the year we were saying "rift.")

"I don't know," Steve said. "The last I heard, she was threatening to dump the whole complicated mess on the Security Council."

"Couldn't they work it out by algebra somehow?" I said.

"Yeah," Perry said, "or logarithms?"

"Yes," I said, darting a quick smile at him, as if we were really clicking, "or logarithms."

David hesitated alongside us, making patterns on the ground with his hoe, not knowing whether he should stop or go past. They looked at him without curiosity. I didn't introduce him.

"It's a scorcher, ain't it!" David said.

"Yes, it's really hot," they said.

"Has it been hot in the city?" I said, as if accommodating the tone of my remark to the stature of his.

"Not bad," they said. "Not so far."

"We always get a good breeze here at night," David said.

There was a pause, as if the real conversation had stopped.

I had been angry with David, and I did it that day the way the city ones did it after anger. That way, you waited until others joined you and then you talked with them. Not making a point of it, as if to show the one you'd quarrelled with that he wasn't the *only* friend you had; but just easily, as if the quarrel had become quite forgotten, now that these people you could really be yourself with were there. And if the quiet one doesn't leave at once, you draw him into the conversation, as if with kindness, from time to time; but you listen to what he says with patience, and sometimes after he has spoken you let his words hang in the silence a minute before you reply, and after awhile he begins to feel like someone trying desperately to cover his large inescapable hands.

They were asking me, why didn't the three of us get some rooms together next year, and cook our own meals?

"We could send you some sauerkraut," David said. We all laughed politely at his little joke. I saw Steve's eyes catch Perry's.

"Now, Dave . . ." I said, tolerantly. There was quite a long silence.

"By the way," I said to Perry, "What brings you two to these hinter parts anyway?"

David stood there, with the selfconsciousness that had made it so hard for him to stop and break into our talk at first making it just as hard, once he had stopped, for him to leave.

"Well, this ain't getting my work done," he said. We let his remark lie where it fell. We didn't help him out in the establishment of anything he said.

He bent over and began to cut the weeds again, but he still couldn't get clean away, because it was a slow business moving up the row with his hoe. The others scarcely glanced after him. I suppose they thought he was the hired man. I still talked their way, for him to hear. I let him believe that the glibness of my mind and theirs was a strangeness between him and people like us that he could never hope to overcome. That he wouldn't fit in with us at all. I put him outside, in the cruellest way it is possible to be put outside.

David, who once when I had cried because they wouldn't let me go to the back field for the cows with him, had felt so badly he'd gone out and broken the handle of my cart—so I'd hate him and wouldn't *want* to go. . . .

That's the mean, rotten way I struck my brother that day.

It wasn't the same after the others had gone that day, as it had been times before when we had quarrelled. He didn't come over and ask me what time it was or something, to break the silence. It was I who had to speak first. I took my hoe over to him and said, "Will you touch her up a little for me with the file, Dave?" But it wasn't like the times I used to borrow his knife.

He said, "Sure"; but he said it too eagerly, and he didn't ask right away about the people who had been there. I hesitated to mention them too. And then after we had both hesitated, it wasn't possible to mention them at all. It wasn't true what I had let him believe that day—that they were my own kind and he was the stranger.

And walking back to the house that night, this thing between us that neither of us could mention lay on our tongues like a weight. He was quiet, without anger or protest, at the blow. And I had shame, which confession could only add to. The consciousness of even the movement of each other's limbs was so taut in us that if our feet had happened to slip and touch on the uneven ground, we'd have been struck with awkwardness beyond description.

Have you ever *really* lain awake the whole night? I did, that one. You know how, if you bruise your finger, it's when you go to bed that it really begins to throb. It was like that with my mind. How could I ever show David it wasn't the real me who had spoken that day—I had done my act so well. You can say, "I'm sorry I struck you, I guess I lost my temper"; but you can't say you're sorry for a thing like what I'd done, without stirring up the shame fresher still. How could my mind show me the answer now, the mind my brother was always so proud of, though he couldn't speak his pride—when it was that mind which I had used as the instrument to strike him!

I wondered if he remembered, that afternoon, the casual way I'd always answered him whenever he asked me things about college. I'd never thought he really cared about knowing. Maybe he had. That was a funny part about David. I had the quicker way with the mind, and still I couldn't feel how it was with him, the way he seemed to know, with a quiet sensing, exactly how it was

58

with me. I wondered if he'd thought that I was putting him off when he asked me those questions. I thought, look Dave, I'd tell you about college now, if you could ask me again. We'd sit all afternoon on the doorstep, pulling the timothy heads from their stalks and talking the easy way.

I wondered if he believed now that if he were in a quarrel with someone *else*, I might not take his side. (And I remembered—Oh Lord, I remembered—how David would always let me fight my own battles with kids my own size; but if any of the older ones so much as laid a finger on me he'd go into the only rages I'd ever seen him show.) I thought foolish things. I tried to console myself with the projection of foolish fictions: there was a war and David went first; because he was the strong one in the flesh and I was the one who had only the thin muscles of the mind.

But I lied to the examiners, and after awhile they took me too. I was small, but when I was angry I was as strong as the others. I was with David when he was in danger now, and so I was strong all the time. And the day David was killed I was right there, and in that last minute when all things are without falseness of any kind, he knew at last that I had been sick for what I had done to him. He knew that I wished we might change places. That the quickness of my mind would be nothing to part with, if it could save *him*. That I was never proud of it, myself, if it stood between us.

I started at the beginning again, making it happen a different way: I saw them when they got out of the car. Before they saw me. I ran down the row to where David was standing and grabbed his arm, with the anger all forgotten. "Dave," I said, "quick—there are some guys I knew at college over at the house and we don't want *them* stuck here all afternoon. Let's get out of sight in the orchard, quick. . . ."

Oh they *did* laugh at David. They said, "Who's your friend?"

"Who's my friend?" I said. "That's my brother. His name is David. You wouldn't know anyone like him. They made him first, out of the muscles and heart and sense—and then they had some pieces of tongue and gut left over and they added a little water and made you. They added quite a bit of water. Would you like him to come over and turn you inside out, to dry? It'd only take a couple of minutes. One to do it, and one to wash his hands afterward. Don't worry, he wouldn't laugh at you. Dave's a gentleman. He wouldn't laugh at that smooth little city-face of yours, Perry, or those little cellar-sprouts on your mind, or that rugged little necktie you're wearing, Steve."

Oh I told them so surely just why their kind wouldn't even move the needle on the scales you'd weigh David in. With such a clean cutting that they wouldn't reply, for all their glibness. They believed it of themselves all right. They were glad to get away from our field quickly. The sharp sword of my mind shone and sang doing it, and I was really proud of its quickness. And then I leaped over the rows eagerly with my hoe, to where David was standing; the song sharp in me almost to tears. The song of one who takes up the cudgel for another with whom he has himself quarrelled, with the bright telling words the other could never in the world have found for himself—

But it was too late to do it that way now. It was foolish to take it out like that on Steve and Perry. They were good enough fellows. They weren't to blame. There was no one to blame but myself. And it would never be the same between David and me again.

The next afternoon the wood saw came. I was so draggy I didn't know how I would ever work. Lift the heavy logs and carry them to the saw table, then lift and thrust, lift and thrust, lift and thrust—without a minute's respite. With the crescendo whine of the whirling saw rising so demandingly between cuts that it seemed it would shatter itself to bits if it were not immediately fed again.

I always dreaded the wood saw. But somehow David had always managed that I got a break in the work now and then, without drawing attention to my weakness. He'd call, "Danny, go get us a dipper of water?" or "Danny, go get the crosscut, will you? We may have to junk some of the big ones." (As if he hadn't left the crosscut saw in the shop purposely.) When he sensed that I was getting intolerably tired, he'd call, "Move her ahead, fuhllas, eh? We're getting too far from the pile." There'd be five minutes or so then, while the others were pushing the machine ahead, and having a smoke maybe before they started up the engine again, that I could get my wind. And somehow, without his planning it in any way that was obvious, when we all fell into our places for the first cut, David would be at the butt end of the logs, next the saw, and I'd be at the light end, on the far side of the pile.

Stan was sawing that day when we started, Rich was throwing away the blocks, David was next the saw, Joe and App were strung along the pile, and I was at the far end. We hadn't sawed more than three or four of the first small wire birches when David threw his head back in a motion for me to come up front.

"Take it, will you?" he shouted at me, above the roar of the engine, "I gotta get a stake for the wheel. Don't cut them too long." The one who was next the saw regulated the length of the block by thrusting the stick ahead just far enough between cuts.

David got the axe and drove a stake down tight against one wheel, to stop the vibration of the machine. I expected him to change jobs with me again as soon as that was done; but when he came back he went to my place at the end of the stick and left me in his.

It was all right while we sawed the birches. They were easy to lift onto the table, and there was a kind of exhilaration in the lightning rhythm of thrust, zing, thrust, zing, thrust, zing—and the transformation of the straggling lengths of trunk into even-lengthed blocks of firewood that flew from Rich's hands and grew into a neat mound before the shop door.

But when we came to the leaden pasture spruces, their weight became hostile, punishing; and the heightening scream of the saw between cuts more demanding. It seemed as if each time I lifted the butt end of one of them from the pile, it was not by strength, but by an effort of will. Then I had the butt of the stick off the pile, with my heart beating very slowly now after having beaten very fast, it was as if I were dragging it to the stable with the pit of my stomach, not my arms. My arms were trembling. Each time Stan tipped the table ahead so the saw could sever the block, I relaxed and let my weight ride with it. But the next instant it was necessary (would it be really impossible this time?) to lift, thrust, again. The others held up their part of the log with hardly any consciousness of its weight. Sometimes David and App would support it at the loop of one elbow and make a mock pretence of cuffing each others' ears with their free arms. David paid no attention to me at all.

We came to the big hemlock. I looked at it, and before I touched it even, I could feel its stupid sickening weight dragging at my stomach.

"Junk it?" I shouted to Dave.

"No," Dave shouted back, "I think we can handle that one all right, can't we, fuhllas?"

I bent over and put my arms around the butt end. I lifted and lifted, but it didn't budge. The saw was waiting, screaming higher and higher, threatening to shatter itself. I lifted again, until everything went black for an instant before my eyes. I couldn't move it an inch off the ground. I straightened up, for my sight to clear. And then I noticed that the others weren't lifting at all. David was motioning them back with his arm.

It was a kind of joke. They were standing there, sort of nudging each other with their grins.

"What's the matter, Dan?" Joe shouted. "Is she nailed down?"

I couldn't even laugh it off. It you weren't brought up in the country, you can't understand what a peculiar sort of shame there is in not being able to take as heavy a hoist as the next one. It was worse still because Joe had shouted. Everything that happened that day was worse still, because everything that was said had to be shouted above the sound of the saw.

They sprang to help me, and somehow I stumbled back and dropped my end of the stick on the saw table. I glanced at David. He was grinning too. I couldn't understand it.

We had to keep turning that one—the force of the saw would die about halfway through. The second or third block, Stan motioned us to wait until the saw had got up speed again. I let my end of the stick rest on the table and relaxed. I motioned to David to come up front.

"I've got sawdust in my eye," I shouted to him. I thought he'd send me into the house to wash my eyes in the eye-cup. He didn't.

"Let's see," he said. He drew my lower lid down. "There's nothing there. It must be just the sweat."

"Okay, fuhllas," Stan shouted. David bounded back to his place at the pile in an exaggerated comic rush. When he passed App, he pointed to his own eyes and sort of smiled. App caught on—the eye business was just an excuse. I couldn't understand it at all.

It got so I could only keep going by thinking about six o'clock. Six o'clock, when this would be over, must come somehow. Nothing could stop it. It got so I turned my face sidewise from the others, because it was twitching uncontrollably, like the tic of a smile that has to be held too long; and I knew it was pale as slush, despite the heat. My second strength came and went. I kept my eyes on the belt, willing it to go off the pulleys, as it had other times we'd sawed; but it didn't. It got so I could only keep going by thinking that when I absolutely *couldn't* stand it any longer, I could ask them, myself, to move the machine ahead; saving that, like a weapon.

"Move her ahead," I shouted at last.

"Move her ahead," David shouted to Stan, "Move her ahead. . . ."

Stan moved to shut off the engine. I took a great deep breath and relaxed.

"No," David shouted, "Don't shut her off . . . unless anyone wants a puff. Anyone tired?" The others shook their heads.

"Will I shut her off?" Stan shouted again.

"No," David shouted. "This stuff's just kindling wood for us fuhllas." He rushed front, worked the stake free in a flash, lifted the tongue of the wagon the machine was resting on, as if it were a match stick.

It wasn't a minute before the wagon was pushed ahead into place, with the saw still running. It wasn't two minutes before the wheels were chocked, the stake driven again, and we back in place for the next cut. My last weapon was gone.

It got so the pile was a looming, leaden, inimical mound of all the weight in the world. It got so the weight of the logs was there all the time in the pit of my stomach, whether I was lifting or not. My temples drew and beat.

Finally it got so I kept lifting at the log on the table, whether the saw was in cut or not, because I couldn't let go. It got so I was suspended somewhere by my arms, with the weight of my body intolerable, but unable to touch the ground with my feet. It got so my body was full of ashes. It got so my will began to tremble as uncontrollably as my arms. It got so I couldn't lift a straw. I motioned for David to come.

"I can't—" I said.

He did something that I wouldn't have believed. He turned and shouted to the others, "Dan's all in, fuhllas. We can finish that little bit all right alone, can't we? All right, Dan, you go in the house."

He needn't have shouted it out like that. He could have sent me to water the calves, or to put hay in to the cow that had been kept in the barn because this was her day.

I held my head down as I took off my leather gloves and walked to the house. But I could see the others out of the corner of my eye. Stan and Rich glanced after me, knowingly, though they hadn't caught what David said; but without much curiosity or concern. I saw David and Joe making a comic battle for each others' caps, even as they held the log. I remembered the night David had taken me on his shoulders when I stumbled on the path from camp and carried me all the rest of the way home; pretending not only to the other kids but to me too that he thought I'd broken a bone in my ankle. So that even with him I needn't have the shame of tiring before the rest. I thought, I understood now. How he must hate me now—

We didn't make much talk with the others at supper. It was on the way down from the barn, with the milk pails in our hands, that he said to me, "Did you make up your mind to live with Perry and Steve next year Dan?"

"No!" I said, as automatically as if a trigger had been pressed—before I stopped to think that this was the first time David had mentioned them. *"Those—?"*

"You crazy old—" He called me a name as old and earthy as the land he hoed. That's what he always called me when it was a hundred per cent perfect between us.

I didn't speak, because tired as I was and so suddenly happy, I couldn't trust my voice. I understood then what had happened this afternoon: how else could he square it between him and me, between me and my conscience, than by doing something as mean to me as I had done to him? How else, since it couldn't be mentioned with words, could he show me that he'd known all the time the falseness of what I'd done, the burden of it afterward—how else, than by doing something as unmentionable to me today and letting me see, by his face now, the falseness and the burden of that?

Did I say it was David who was the clumsy one with anything that couldn't be held in his hands?

LOVE AMONG STRANGERS

The Dream and
the Triumph

It was that March when, as people said, Chris and Mary Redmond had "just got where they could live," that Chris put the fork tine into his heel, bedding the horses. He thought nothing of it until he noticed the blood on his sock that night. Chris's face was lined with the big tracks of the big feelings only, no fretwork of the petty worries at all.

But even as Mary was bathing the tiny wound and he was laughing at her suggestion of a bread poultice, the tetanus germ was already entrenched. Mary was a small woman who took stature from her spirited expression, touched with something universal in its quiet moments.

"Let's see," Chris said, "when did we hear from Paul last?" He said this almost every night, just before he went to bed.

Paul was their grandson. They had brought him up from the time he was orphaned at ten.

He was away now at the city's engineering college. Even as a child he'd taken the mathematician's almost sensuous delight in surprising from a thing the equations that ran like hidden bones through it. The year he'd gone to high school in town and won the scholarship Mary hadn't been able to afford any new clothes. But she'd studied his grammar nights after her work was done so that she wouldn't say anything too wrong at graduation time to embarrass him.

"Ah, this is Wednesday," she said to Chris now. "No, it's Thursday, isn't it? I don't know why, but I seem to have lost a day this week. Well, then, we heard from him on Monday. Now, if that heel bothers you any. . . ."

"*It's* all right," Chris said. "The heat makes it feel good. Next time you write you better slip a few dollars into the envelope. I wouldn't want to think of him bein' strapped up there. And you know Paul . . . he wouldn't say, if. . . ."

"I know," Mary said.

"D'ya mind the time he lost the new purse you give him for Christmas," Chris said, "and he wouldn't let on and you got him another one just like it and pretended you'd found it where he was coasting, and you never let on either?"

"I remember," Mary said. "I don't believe he ever knew the difference." She smiled. "I must ask him about that when he comes home in May."

When Saturday's train passed over the river bridge, then blew for the station in town, Paul felt his nerves tauten. All along in the train he'd had only one thought, if I'd been home it wouldn't have happened. Bedding the horses, that was always my job. Your job . . . your job . . . your job . . . the train wheels accused him.

The first familiar thing that caught his eye when he stepped onto the station platform was the old doctor's coonskin coat.

He put his suitcases in the back of the doctor's sleigh. But he didn't ask him any questions. Somehow he couldn't bear to, at the dingy station, in the town itself, where Chris has always seemed to be years rather than a few miles away from home.

When they came to the brook where Chris always stopped the horse for water and told him to "reach back in the big brown bag there" if he wanted some candy, Paul said, "How is he?"

"Well," the doctor said, "I thought it'd make your grandmother feel better if I came out again today, but. . . ." He shook his head.

The horse slowed to a stop. Paul's eyes fell on the skates tied to the outside of his suitcase of books. Somehow in the country men never seemed to skate after life stopped its circling just above their shoulders and settled on them. He knew he would never skate much again.

The next few days Paul could never get quite distinct. There are no equations for feeling.

Each time his thought tried to get things clear, a series of distracting images would block its path: His grandmother's Sunday dress and her awakened-in-the-night face that first afternoon when he and the doctor came into the house. His grandfather, raising himself on one elbow in bed, as if he couldn't talk unless his eyes were on the same level as the hearer's. His saying, with pain wavering his face like puffs of breeze on a lamp flame when the door blows open, "Ye'll find the axe where I started to clear the alders, Paul, and Fridays I always lay out to change the straw in the hens' nests." And, later, his grandmother's face, as her hand polished the nickel bar on the side of the stove, back and forth, back and forth, as she said, "No, it was Thursday. I don't know, I seem to have lost a day last week."

There was that final moment in the bedroom when three people there became two people there, unalterably, and nothing moved but the curtain, in and out a little, suddenly, like a sigh. And the moment when Mary first touched the pressing iron to Chris's good suit which, though he was a man to whom clothes mattered not at all, must have had *something* in its pattern that made him choose it rather than another.

"Paul," Mary said the second night after the funeral, "what made you bring home all your books and everything . . . your skates and everything? You can't stay here. There's nothing here for anyone like you."

Nothing in Mary's tone had bid for pity or special consideration. It was merely the drained reasoning voice of one who has always been a foundation block in the household before, now feeling a helpless guilt for being there only as the hinge on which a cold practical decision, which none of them had ever dreamed of having to face, turned.

Paul couldn't answer. His tongue seemed out of connection with his mind.

As though to confront him with fact upon disrupting fact, his eyes staring out the window fell on Molly Gladwin walking down the road. If anyone had ever given Paul the word "girl" in one of those association tests, he'd have answered instantly, "Molly Gladwin."

There had always been a kind of unformed anchoring thought in the back of his mind that he and Molly might be married as soon as he'd finished his education. But now. . . .

"We could sell the stock," Mary said. "And I could manage all right."

And have it no less still all afternoon than when you blew out the lamp and went to bed? Never cooking anything to be divided. To have your thoughts creep back into your mind from the touch of table and chair which need two faces in the room to have a face of their own? And sometimes to sit, after your needle was put away, and stare mindlessly at your own hands and feet?

He was still silent.

"Or maybe I could go with Em," Mary said.

"You're not going with Aunt Em!" Paul exclaimed.

She had wanted to take *him* when both his parents died that same week of the black diphtheria. He would never forget his helpless dismay at the thought of going to live with Aunt Em and Uncle How. Nor would he ever forget his grandmother's gentle insistence, though without a word ever having passed between them, that this must not be.

And now she wasn't going there! It wasn't that Aunt Em and Uncle How weren't good as gold, but they only put one stick of wood in the stove at a time, and they never did the least thing that surprised themselves or anyone else, and even the air in their house seemed to be yellowing with disuse.

"You're not going with Aunt Em," he said. "I can tell you that!"

Mary took a long breath. "Maybe we should . . . sell the place . . . then. And I could. . . ." She didn't finish the sentence.

"Sell the place." He knew what it had cost her even to pronounce the words. This place was the very rivers and mountains in the geography of her thoughts and feelings, and away from it they would crumble and decay.

"I'm not going back to the city," he said. "I can make a living here all right."

"Look at your hands," Mary said gently. "There's nothing but hard work here, Paul."

Well, his hands had toughened now. They stripped down the low branches of a standing tree with the axe or ribboned a perfect furrow with the plough, as if axe and plough were the only tools scaled to them. His dark face came to have the same countryman's grip in it as Chris's had had.

Yet the shadow of Paul's city life still lingered in him, disconcerting him. What kind, what better kind, of someone else might he have been if he had stayed there?

And Mary knew how he felt. Nothing either did for the other was in the least grudging. And to each the other was the projection of himself where injury or slight would sting sharpest. But he was restless, and she was beholden. That was always there.

And so it came to be an area of constraint as tender and diffused as a blind boil.

They fell into the habit of examining beforehand whatever they said or did in each other's presence, to inhibit it if it threatened to touch on this sore spot. They couldn't seem to communicate a piece of news to each other with normal zest. One would have to lay it down as if he weren't looking, and the other pick it up slowly by the edge. A joke between them became impossible.

And though they didn't lie in wait to score off each other, they did fall into the habit of saying things like, "No wonder you have a cold. You never brush the snow off your clothes when you come into the house." Or, "You left the cellar door open last night." Or, "I thought you said you weren't *going* to wash today."

Most crippling of all, each knew (and knew that the other knew) that the prospect was a downhill one. Mary lived under the shadow of the day when she must ask his help inside the house, when she could no longer manage the care of her own person. And Paul fell into the awful stoicism that borrows no enlargement whatever for the things of today from the expectations of tomorrow.

Finally, as it was bound to, there came the afternoon when the blighting accusation was spoken and the indelible response was put into words.

It had been for Paul one of those days of clenched, grinding mood which everyone knows occasionally. When there is a conspiracy among even trifles to frustrate you.

He had overslept. The single gust of wind that morning came at the very second the butt of the big spruce was severed, and took it into the thicket. He couldn't have found a rock in that part of the woods if he'd searched for one, but his axe found one all right. His watch stoiped and tricked him into arriving home just too late to catch the dairyman he'd been waiting weeks to see.

And—Molly Gladwin. Her name stung suddenly in his mind like a spot these irritations had scraped the scab off so that the fresh blood came. Everyone else had a wife. . . .

When he stepped into the kitchen half an hour past dinnertime, Mary said to him, "I thought you were coming home early, Paul. The dairyman stopped in to see you, but he couldn't wait."

"What the hell difference does it make?" he flashed out at her. "Anyone buried in this damn . . . all his life . . . poor as a church mouse . . . working your heart out for a few dollars. . . ."

He didn't know where the false words came from, how they slipped past his guard. They made no sense as an answer to her question.

Mary caught her breath. "Well, Paul," she said, "old people have to live till they die. Do you ever stop to think what it's like for me? You'll be old some day."

They turned away from each other's face, and each looked as if he wished he could turn away from his own. There is nothing so terrible as the silence after words like that in a country kitchen. There is nothing as terrible as sitting at the table and swallowing your food (it was spareribs; it was to have been special) after a silence like that.

It was the very next morning when Paul was fishing in the button box on the shelf for a piece of carpenter's chalk that the faded clipping tucked behind it fluttered on the couch.

He bent to retrieve it, and Mary said quickly, "Give it here and I'll put it in the stove. Trash collects so."

He passed it to her and she burned it. But he couldn't help noticing the big black headlines: DELICATE OPERATION RESTORES SIGHT TO 90-YEAR-OLD WOMAN.

Why did she read so little now and sew so little? The answer came to him like a blow. He narrowed his own lids and made the kitchen go like a snapshot taken when it is almost dark. To have it every minute of the day like that. . . .

He desperately wanted to say something, but how could he, with the punishing memory of what he'd said yesterday still so raw?

The next day at dinner he forced himself to bring it up, obliquely.

"Why don't you go into town someday and have your eyes looked after?" he said. "Those old glasses must be. . . ."

She hesitated. "I did," she said. "The day I took in the mats."

Yes, she must have. He remembered how that day when she'd come home she'd stood on the porch with her packages still in her arms and looked about the fields for several minutes, like someone committing them to memory before a long journey.

"What did he say?" he said.

"Oh," she said, "he didn't tell me much of anything different. You'll have to season that squash yourself," she added quickly, "I forgot the salt."

When she went outside to feed the hens, Paul phoned the doctor. Yes. Yes, both of them. Yes, progressive. Maybe six months . . . a year . . . it was hard to tell. Well, yes, sometimes they could . . . there was this brilliant new eye surgeon in the city. . . .

Paul thanked him. The city . . . at her age it would seem like the ends of the earth to her. A hospital . . . the word which all country people recoil from. The expense . . . she'd never in the world consent to take his money. *Never*, after what he'd said.

And that evening he knew the answer to the question which two days ago his anger had flushed from behind her face. "Do you ever stop to think what it's like for me?"

What must it be like for the old?

Was being old anything they could help? Was it their fault that people were made half angry by whatever it is in people which makes them half angry at anything they might, if they let themselves consider it, pity?

He couldn't get to sleep that night. He turned one eye against the pillow and darkened the other with the palm of his hand, trying for sleep that way. But it was no use.

Mary had always liked to be in some small way somebody particular. It had nothing to do with pride, or ambition, or dissatisfaction with the country-woman's lot. But any little thing that won her recognition by outside standards (though she herself might know it was a silly thing to put any real stock in) gave her a curious glow.

She had never had but one ring with a stone in it, and it was not valuable. But she knew instinctively which things might be old and plain but still beautiful, as she knew which ones might be expensive but still just cheap. And whenever a stranger was coming she would slip it on her finger and hold that hand uppermost in her lap. She knew how to set her table just right for her kind of house, with no hint of imitation from a magazine page. She had, in her Bible, the letter the judge of a handwriting contest had written her once, awarding her first prize of five dollars and saying that she "showed an artist's touch." She still had the five-dollar bill, too.

She had kept in a twist of tissue paper in her top bureau drawer the little gold hoop which a tourist, stopping for a drink at the well, had impulsively taken off her own hair and put onto Mary's because she said—and Mary could tell that the spirit of the action was in no way rude or patronizing—it was just the thing to make Mary look like a character study for Renoir.

He got up and lit a cigarette.

He knew that just beneath her consciousness had always been the feeling that her life would reach some extraordinary little distinction, the thing she'd be remembered by. But instead of her life coming to any climax, it was like a room that gets silent and more silent as the fire stills and stills. It was as if a child's birthday were coming up when of course some plan must be underway, unknown to him, to put something splendid into his hand, and yet no one was planning anything at all.

He sat on the side of the bed, his last cigarette gone, alone in the deaf night-stillness that rings in your ears with every note of how you may have failed someone.

She was never to blame about Molly, he thought. It was the doubts my own imagination cast up. How would she and Molly get along? Would it be fair to either of them? And, deeper than that, it was my own crippling doubt. If you didn't know what kind of life was going to be yours later on, how could you tell which kind of girl you should ask to share it?

She didn't deny me wife and children. If there was ever any question of denial, I denied them to her—the family stir which should be there to shield anyone old from the bare still face of things as they are.

She rescued me from Aunt Em, but she never crowded me, like Aunt Em would have. She never put out a single tendril around my independence even then. . . .

His thoughts had seemed only to roil and writhe, but the glancing memory of Mary's handwriting prize must have struck root in Paul's brain. Otherwise a recurring notice in the farm periodical they subscribed to would have snagged his interest for the first time that very next night.

It was the announcement of a much bigger contest. Whoever the editors decided had sent in the best account of "My Favourite Memory" would receive five brand-new, hundred-dollar bills.

He had a sudden wild notion. If Mary had that much money which she'd won herself. . . . Why couldn't he fake it?

"Here's something," he said to her awkwardly. Speech between them still came like a startling sound. He read her the details. "Why don't you try it? You could think it up and I could write it down for you."

She gave the idea that particular smile you accord the preposterous. "Paul!" she said. "You know I could never put anything together that would. . . ."

But the next night when he said again, "Why don't you try that contest?" she hesitated a minute, and then she said, "Well . . . I suppose we wouldn't lose anything but the stamp, would we?"

She must have kept her mind on it all the next day. For that evening, diffidently, she brought out a whole sheaf of recollections to pick from.

He found it curiously hurting to see her so unsuspectingly serious over a choice. To know that, however she poked fun at her folly in presuming to chance this thing, she had a secret little hope in what she was doing nevertheless. But if his plan worked. . . .

"My husband was working away the day I lost my wedding ring," the memory she finally decided on went. "He didn't like to leave me with the chores, but that was the first year we were married and there was hardly any money. I hated to tell him when he came home. I was never afraid to tell him anything, but here I'd been supposed to be helping him out, and the ring had cost twenty dollars. I tried to make out I didn't mind as much as I did, but I felt heartbroken and naked without it.

"I was pretty sure I had lost it in the barn. We looked all through the barn. In the linter. In the feedbin. In the chaff on the barn floor. And he went over the whole haymow as cautious as a kitten poking the tines of the fork down through the loose hay and listening for a clink. We couldn't find it anywhere.

"He had a heifer he was raising for an extra cow. One day he said, 'I think I'll beef that heifer. She wouldn't make much of a cow.' I said, 'No, Chris, don't sell her, the money'll only go. Trade her in on another cow.' 'No,' he said, 'I think I'll sell her. One cow's enough for you to look after when I'm away so much.' I thought, he's going to beef her and sell her and buy me another ring. We couldn't afford it. But I didn't care to tell him not to spend the money that way because, if that wasn't what he had in mind, then he might think he had to.

"He killed the heifer and when they opened her, there was the ring, lodged in that part of her stomach they call the book because it looks a little like the leaves of a book. It must have got into her bran and middlings when I was swishing them up together in her feedbox and she'd swallowed it. It hadn't hurt her a bit.

"I remember the look on his face when he came in the door that day with his closed fist stuck out, and when he spread his fingers open and there was the ring in the palm of his hand.

"And I remember what he said when he slipped it on my finger again. 'This should be a lesson to us. We must never be afraid to part with something we need, to buy something we. . . .'

He didn't finish, but I knew what he meant. And we never were."

The next day in town Paul went to the bank, and miraculously they did have five new hundred-dollar bills. It seemed like a blessing on his plan. The withdrawal almost emptied his account but he was reminded of Chris's words about the ring. The coincidence seemed like a good omen.

Then he bought an airmail envelope and stamp and a pad of typewriter paper. He used the typewriter at the library. He wrote, "Dear Mrs. Redmond: It is our great pleasure to inform you that your entry has been chosen as the best of all submitted in our recent contest. First-prize money is enclosed, with our heartiest congratulations."

He folded the sheet and put it into the envelope, with the bills, and sealed and stamped the envelope. It gave him a sudden pang to realize that all this forging of detail was probably needless. She could hardly tell one set of words, or one envelope, from another now.

She would need new clothes. He hesitated twice at the door of Chapman's Ladies' Wear and twice passed on.

The third trip by, he glanced through the window and saw Molly Gladwin standing beside the long counter.

With that heightened awareness you feel just after the ice of some daring project has first been broken, he seemed to be seeing her truly for the first time. He seemed to catch in this glimpse of her generous brown-eyed face, with that delicacy just below the skin which minimizes each feature and is more like the delicacy of hands, the essence of her. As if in a frame. For no good reason, it seemed to him to be a face that must be protected from ever going small with slight.

He went inside.

"I . . ." he said to her. "She needs a new dress and coat and hat and shoes. I thought maybe you. . . . How would that hat do, there in the window?"

Molly turned her back to the saleswoman and grimaced at him, just barely shaking her head and half laughing.

"No," she whispered, drawing him away from the counter, "Paul! That's kind of an old funeral hat. She wants something with . . . there, more like that one . . . with a little"—she made a motion with her hands—"in the front, and just a tiny little veil."

And when it came to the dress, she said, "No, Paul, she doesn't want a black dress. She wants a pattern, maybe great big flowers even, with some white around the neck. . . ."

He had a picture of her and Mary deep in that special climate of settling on what kind of clothing looked best on each other and laughing at him for the mystery he found the whole thing. Or in that other special climate of planning the feminine touches inside a house which a man may find pleasant but must pretend not to notice except almost grudgingly, and which he'd envision wildly wrong if he were asked for suggestions.

He paid for the things and arranged to leave them at the store until the time came, he hoped, for Mary's trip to the city.

On an impulse he confided his plan to Molly. "Well, bless you . . ." she said.

When he closed the door on the way out, he caught another glimpse of her, back at the counter again.

Her hand lay perfectly still on the bolt of cloth the saleswoman had rolled out for her. She was looking at him with that absorbed expression which gives such a wonderful feeling to anyone at whom no one else ever turns his head when the conversation is over and he has walked away.

Of all the people he knew, Molly alone could lighten his plaguing intentness instantly. And afterward he always felt like holding his head straighter and smiling at people and taking deeper breaths and longer steps.

The afternoon Paul slipped the airmail envelope inside the newspaper at the mailbox, Mary was trying to patch an apron.

"Paul," she said, "before you look at the paper, could you thread this needle for me? The eye seems to be so fine."

"In a minute," he said, opening the paper, smiling. "Look at this first."

She took the envelope in her hand and her hands began to tremble.

"Paul," she said, and her voice sounded frightened almost, "it isn't . . . is it? Open it."

"No," he said, "you open it. It's for you."

She opened the envelope and when she unfolded the sheet of paper, the bills fell into her lap.

He saw that she couldn't speak, and he picked up the sheet of paper to read out what was on it.

"Oh, Paul!" she cried. "I never *dreamed* . . . did you?" She put her apron to her eyes.

"Now, don't . . ." he said.

"I can't help it," she said, wresting the tremour of her voice into a shaky little laugh. "I'm such a fool when anything like this happens!" Her face shone. "Now you can get. . . . There's so many things."

"I don't need anything," he said. "What that money's going for is to have your eyes seen to!"

She shook her head. "No," she said, "no. There's so many things we need."

Paul spoke with mock sternness. "Do you remember what Grandfather said, about what you need and what you . . . ?"

She had to try hard, not to cry again. The way it is when mention is made of some affliction you have borne silently and without hope, which suddenly seems almost like a friend, now that a miraculous way is open to release from it.

"Of course, I suppose . . ." she spoke hesitantly, as if she were stating aloud to herself what she must have stated silently to herself time and time again, though knowing she could never give in to her own argument, ". . . if I let them go and was to get so I couldn't. . . ."

She stopped again. Her voice could only support so many words at a time. "It almost seems like this was sent, doesn't it? I believe in those things!"

Paul wouldn't have credited that anything could so alter the tempo of their living. Even the days seemed to have a new spring in their step.

Mary put up no real resistance to any of the things he had expected she would resist. Neither to her new clothes, now that she believed her own money had bought them, nor to the trip, nor to the hospital.

Molly came over and showed her at just what angle the hat should be worn, and he heard them consulting about what she should or should nor pack in her suitcase. (She'd have hated to take her own hairbrush if that should prove to be a homeliness which marked her as unused to the knowledge of outside ways.)

Of the trip he'd thought she'd say, "It seems like such an undertaking at my age." Instead, she said, "The plane from Greenwood would take us there in a couple of hours, but I suppose it'd cost a lot more that way, wouldn't it?" And he thought how many small luxuries and excitements, I've always taken for granted would have no claim on her, she must have had a secret little weakness for all along.

He was determined that nothing should spoil it for her. He gave her no hint of his one terrible misgiving. A taste of the city, and what fresh restlessness would he have to battle all over again when he came back home?

But there was no denying it. Each time she said jubilantly, "It will be a change for you too, Paul," it came to the surface like a treacherous fin.

It was only in aftersight that Paul recognized those times when the words "proud" and "exultant" had come closest to pronouncing their own name explicitly in his consciousness.

He was proud of Mary in the plane. Nothing about her pointed or exclaimed. You'd never have guessed that this flight might not be something quite usual for her. But he knew she was thinking, I am almost eighty years old and I am flying in an airplane and everyone is giving me a special smile.

He was proud of her in the surgeon's office.

The surgeon, who had that particular gentleness so often associated with great strength, came down from his doctor's eminence and balanced the grave risks and the tempting hopes for her as concernedly as if she were a member of his own family. She gave him her decision with a single nod of her head—no tears, not one—and a quick trusting grasp of his hand.

He was proud of her in the hospital room.

There the nurses kidded her ("The little one wanted to put lipstick on me today!"), asked her if they could try parting her hair on the other side just to see how it looked, made no secret to her of the fact that she was their favourite and bravest and most extraordinary patient, and confided to her little personal problems of their own. In an innocent and curiously affecting way, it was like a little court to her.

He was proud of her all that long punishing afternoon when all the fantastic contrivances of medical science up to this moment and all the magic of the surgeon's hands had learned up to now were focused on the face that flinched only by a moment's twitch of her smile when the needles stabbed.

He was exultant for her that last day of all in the surgeon's office. As she read down the letters of the chart, while the gentle surgeon smiled deeper and deeper with each line.

She read them proudly and exultantly, as if she were passing her hand over a face believed lost. And then, yes, the two pardonable tears. And once more the impulsive touch, almost reverent now with more of thankfulness than there had been even of trusting before, on both her deliverer's miraculous hands.

"Isn't it odd, Dr. Key!" she said, smiling just right to discount the sentiment of her remark, "you told me things might be a little blurry at first, and your face does seem to have a sort of halo around it."

And right then the doctor made her the gift almost equal to his gift of sight.

He told her her case was so unique he was writing it up for an international medical journal. He would send her a copy.

"Mary Redmond." Her own name in learned print! Circulating all over the world! At last she'd been turned from a crowd-face into somebody particular!

Now her life wouldn't just thin away, absolutely unexceptional. Now she'd have this little fund of special notice, like a small treasure she could carry around in her pocket to touch reassuringly whenever she wished.

"You know I'm almost eighty," she said gently.

"I know," the doctor said, smiling at her that same special smile which the people in the plane had given her. "That's just it!"

The success of Mary's operation Paul had been prepared to rejoice in.

What he'd been totally unprepared for was the bloodless operation on his own vision. Face to face with this place where he'd expected to see everywhere he turned the torturing ghost of his other possible life, he was unbearably homesick. It was as simple as that.

Here where you left no track, where almost everyone was servant to something, where the memory of you stopped with your breath, he longed to be back where you could see the paths your feet had made on the yielding earth. Where your only masters were sun and storm. Where in your neighbours' registry of deeds any little individuality you'd ever achieved was perpetually recorded. And where your little kingdom would always be known as "the Paul Redmond place" as long as the windows of your house still looked out on the spot where you lay. It struck him that intensely.

A letter had come from Molly. He thought, with an unaccountable tenderness, I've never seen my name in her handwriting before.

He thought, she could never fit into the mould that seems to pattern most of these sure-faced wives here. I was right about that. But she has the one thing most of them haven't, the kind of understanding that's a passport anywhere that matters.

He had that wonderful feeling you have when it suddenly dawns on you that you really love someone, the feeling that, between you, an insight into everything is possible. He could hardly wait to tell her how. . . .

But that is Paul's story. This is Mary's.

There are two pictures of Mary that tell the rest of her story better than words.

One, a city reporter took of her for his newspaper the day before she left. She has the little gold hoop on her hair and the smile on her face honestly does give her the look of a Renoir. The smile was still on her face from having just said to Paul, though the contest itself she didn't mention, "Paul, do you remember the time you lost your purse and I pretended I came across it where you'd been coasting? Did *you* ever suspect the difference later?"

The other—and perhaps a better one still—was taken this last month. With Paul, Jr. A child with a quite ordinary face. But you can see by the way she looks at him that she's sure he'll be somebody. Really somebody, for all of them.

In the country, it doesn't matter in the least which member of the family that happens to be.

A Present for Miss Merriam

There is nothing as still as a country schoolroom when only a stray laugh carries back to it from the children who have just left for the new kingdom of sleds and skates.

Miss Merriam had never felt the stillness so strongly before. It was the last morning of school before the Christmas holidays. The tree had seemed to have an evening glow while the children were there and the gifts were being distributed. Now they were gone, it had only a daylight blankness. The air of the room had the hollow smell of chalk and forgotten books.

She began to tidy up. The floor about her desk was littered with the wrappings of their gifts for her: the handkerchiefs, the cakes of toilet soap, the boxes of stationery. She gathered the wrappings and put them into the stove. She smiled to herself. Parents seemed to think a teacher had no other functions than to write a letter or wash her face or have a cold.

Well, *have* I? she thought.

It was one of those sudden self-questionings which seemed to stab her oftener lately. She would see a woman surreptitiously moisten a finger at her lips and perfect her child's curls before admitting a visitor, then make an elaborate pretence of believing that her child was no handsomer than anyone else's. Or maybe, from the road, she'd glimpse movement behind a lighted window, though no sound came to her. Or, try not to as she would, she might find herself ready too soon, and arriving earlier than anyone else, at anything that was going on. Sometimes then, she'd feel as if something had given way beneath her. She'd feel bleak and frightened, the way you do when you oversleep an afternoon nap into the dusk, and for a second when you awake you don't know where you are or how much time has gone irretrievably by.

She was still young . . . well, thirty-three certainly wasn't *old*. When she looked in the mirror *before* a party, her gentle face, though plain, would have such a careless "evening" expression that sometimes she'd feel like smiling back at herself. But why, looking in a mirror at the party itself, would she have a foolish wish that some feature could be a little haphazard, out of balance? Why did she have the feeling lately that beneath her own face, another stiffer one was accreting, to which her own would gradually conform?

She dusted off the top of her desk, and aligned the small globe and the dictionary and the bell neatly along the far edge. Then, as if in some vague sort of desperation, she shoved the globe a little slantwise.

She took the register from her desk and inked in the daily attendance. When she came to Robert Fairfield's name, she felt a momentary pang. Bobby—her favourite—was the only child who hadn't brought her anything.

But of course not. How could she expect a present from Bobby? Who was there to remind him of it?

And, come to think, he'd seemed pretty bored with the whole affair anyway. Though that might be only pose. When something was going on that he couldn't join on the same footing as the others, he affected a studied adult indifference which moved her more, somehow, than any sort of wistfulness. You seldom knew what he was thinking. His face didn't suggest an imaginative child. But when she'd asked them yesterday to make up some little "composition" about Christmas, the others' stubby sentences had all been about Santa Claus and toys: his had been about a "lovely lady, with jewels on." His mother was dead.

She turned at a step in the porch. As if her thought had summoned him, there he was, standing in the door. The look of indifference was almost a frown. He took out a tiny box from his reefer pocket.

"I forgot your present this morning," he said abruptly.

She didn't know which struck her hardest: the clumsy wrapping, with the seals only half stuck; or the transparency of a child who never doubts that his little prevarication has been taken at face value. Obviously, whatever was in the box was something he'd been afraid the other children might laugh at.

"Why, Bobby!" she exclaimed, peering as if with intolerable curiosity at the box. "What can it be?" She held the box up to her ear and shook it. She made a mock grimace of utter puzzlement. "Tiddley-winks?"

He had to giggle. "No," he said.

He couldn't keep the eagerness out of his face when she began to undo the package. Then, just before she lifted off the cover, he said suddenly, "Don't you want me to clean off the blackboard for you?"

"Why, yes," she said, "you can if you like."

He picked up the eraser. But he stood sidewise to the blackboard, keeping the desk in one corner of his eye.

It wasn't anything in the least like a cake of soap or a hand-kerchief. It was a pair of beaten copper earrings. They were of hopelessly extravagant design (for me, she thought) . . . but to a child, searching through the catalogue, they must have seemed like the very essence of elegance. For a second she couldn't speak. He began to rub the blackboard furiously with the eraser.

"They had 'em with pearls too," he said, in a let-down voice.

She knew he'd expected her to exclaim immediately. "But. . . ."

"Oh no . . . these," she faltered. "They just took my breath, that's all. I never thought of such. . . ."

He came over to the desk. He realized now that she was truly overwhelmed, even though he mistook the reason.

"Them was a little more than the pearl ones," he couldn't help adding.

"They're beautiful," she said. "They're the nicest thing I ever. . . ."

"Maybe you *got* earrings," he said, protracting the thing now as long as he could.

"*No*," she said, "I haven't."

"You can change 'em if you don't like 'em," he said. "The slip's in the bottom there."

She knew what he was thinking. If she didn't like them! As if anyone wouldn't like anything as splendid as that! But it wouldn't hurt to mention the slip, so she could see they weren't just old ten-cent ones.

"*Change* them?" she cried. "Look!"

She slipped them onto her ears. His face broke into a great awed smile. "Gee," he said. "They just fit, don't they! They make you look. . . ."

Then the elaborate indifference came back as suddenly as it had left. "I just noticed the jewellery page in the catalogue," he said casually, "and I thought. . . ." He almost darted out the door.

Helen Merriam sat perfectly still for a second. Then, without knowing why, she found herself with her head in her arm, crying. She hadn't realized, until these first tears came, that she'd felt like crying all morning. But she was released enough in a few minutes to stop short and laugh at herself.

She wondered if she should mention the earrings to Bobby's father when she stopped in this morning to have him sign her returns; he was the secretary. She really *should* thank him too, he must have paid for them. But, except with Bobby, he was such a withdrawn man, even for Grenville. And whenever he and she were alone together—when she dropped in to pick up her salary installments; when he came to the schoolhouse, after hours, to fix a desk or a doorknob or the stovepipe; or when they stopped opposite each other in a Paul Jones at one of the rare dances he showed up at—there was a curious awkwardness between them, more than the ordinary awkwardness between two shy and quiet people.

You could tell a house with no woman in it the minute you stepped inside, she thought. There should be a plant in that alcove, there should be the smell of a cake just baked, or of something just washed or scrubbed. There should be something lying half-finished somewhere: mending, or knitting, or a garment.

Not that Chris Fairfield didn't manage far better than most men would have. The house was perfectly tidy, and Bobby never had the urchin look which most children do who are dressed by a man.

Chris was rather an unusual man for here. He'd gone through Grade Ten, and read everything he could get his hands on. (The neighbours all brought him their "papers" to fill out.) His large hands seemed incongruous in connection with anything subtler than a plough. But she'd seen a tiny statuette of Bobby he'd carved from a block of peartree wood. He hadn't made it an exact copy, but he'd known just which details to exaggerate a little, to catch Bobby's nature more accurately than a photograph.

He and Bobby were in the front room, trimming the tree. They too use up the last-minute things too early, she thought because there is nothing to postpone them. They didn't hear her enter the kitchen.

"Walk right in," she called. She hated the prim facetiousness of her remark. But it was the sort of thing which always seemed to come out when most she wanted to sound natural.

"Oh . . ." Chris called back. "Is that you, Miss Merriam?"

"Is that you, Miss Merriam?" Bobby echoed. "Come see our tree."

Chris was in the kitchen doorway by that time. He had the almost Scandinavian kind of rugged blondness which makes a man look surprisingly young in dark clothes (and, in his case, so surprisingly at home in good ones).

"Oh, never mind your galoshes," he said.

She straightened up as abruptly as if his tone had been peremptory. She felt more awkward with him today than she ever had. She thought of the earrings. He too seeed more awkward than usual. Perhaps he was thinking about them also. She knew she couldn't mention them.

In the frontroom, though it was large, it seemed as if each must watch carefully before moving, lest they bump into each other.

The tree was a perfect fir. He and Bobby had hung oranges

and tinsel cord on the boughs, and it seemed as if Christmas had really been brought into the room from outdoors. The incarnate smell of the oranges and the fir were like the true breath of the gentle mystery. But here, as with the small tree in her boardinghouse room, she had the feeling that the tree was abating some of its presence for being so privately, almost defensively, possessed.

"Why, it's a beauty," she exclaimed.

"Oh, I don't know about that," Chris said diffidently. "We've no ornaments this year. I guess something got packed on top of them and broke off that little stem thing."

"But that can be fixed," she said. "Just take a bit of match stick and tie some red cord around the middle and. . . ."

"Show us," Bobby interrupted eagerly, "will you?"

She showed them how you dropped the stick straight inside the globe affair, then worked it into a crosswise position to form a support.

"Now that's an idea," Chris said.

Bobby raced to the kitchen for more matches.

"You do these ones, dad," he said, "and I'll do these, and Miss Merriam can do those. Or, no . . . *I* tell you . . . you two *do* 'em, and I'll hang 'em on, eh?"

They obeyed his enthusiasm without comment, as if it gave them a curious docility.

Bobby'd test one against a bough and say, "There, Miss Merriam, do you think?" "Well," she'd say, "there . . . or over just a speck, maybe." Or his father might say, "Think you should have two red ones so close together there, Bobby?" With everyone's hands busy, the room seemed to relax.

Then she and Chris reached for the same ornament at the same time. Suddenly she had an acute consciousness of sitting there with her hat and coat and galoshes on.

"I brought my returns," she said abruptly.

"Oh yes," Chris said. He stood up.

"But we're not near done," Bobby said, dismayed.

"I guess we can finish all right now, son," Chris said. "Miss Merriam's got other things to do."

"Oh, couldn't you just . . ." Bobby began. But she had risen too.

She had nothing else to do. There was no way you could synthesize that frantic rush the other women deplored, and which she envied so. She always had her cards mailed, and everything ready a week ahead. But how could she admit that?

Bobby began to hang the rest of the ornaments slowly, and any old place. She and Chris went back to the kitchen.

"I hope you have a good holiday in Halifax," he said, when she was ready to go.

"Thank you," she said.

(Now who'd have thought he'd remember my plans for Christmas, she thought. She'd forgotten mentioning them to him herself. But his remembering gave her a strange pleasure. She was so used to hearing the others say, "Oh, yes, I believe you *did* tell me that.")

"Will you be back for Christmas Eve?"

"No," she said. "Not until Christmas Day." She couldn't tell him why.

If you had no family of your own, you'd think that to spend Christmas with an aunt, or at least at your boardinghouse where you knew the people, would be better than spending it among strangers. But it wasn't, for her. The last few years, she didn't know just why, those hours between first lamplight and twelve o'clock on this one day of the year were ones she couldn't bear to spend anywhere she was known. With friends, whose behaviour was so unfettered by the *predictable*. Who (no matter how kindly they included you in their circle) each had someone special they looked at, openly, in the way they'd felt about them only obscurely, throughout the year. Someone already there. Or someone they were waiting for, to come. Or someone they might make some spontaneous plan, at the last minute, to go surprise, themselves. . . .

She went to the city a day or two ahead, and spent Christmas Eve in her hotel room. Not really unhappy . . . just so long as she could shut out the carols. The others only half heard them, or were bored with them because they'd heard them so much. For her they carried an awful evocativeness of something, she couldn't say just what.

Christmas Day itself she didn't mind. At the stroke of twelve, everything was all right again.

"I hope you have a nice Christmas too," she said. The stilted sentence almost angered her. She didn't mean to sound like that. She wasn't *like* that.

"Oh, yes," he said. "It'll be quiet, but"—he hesitated—"I often think I should take Bobby to the city some Christmas time, to see the stores and everything."

She had a sudden impulse. "Why couldn't he come with me?" she said.

"Oh, no, no," he said. "I wasn't hinting. I just meant maybe sometime he and I. . . ."

"I know," she said. "But he could come."

"Where?" Bobby said suddenly from the doorway. He had heard his name.

Chris tried to turn it into a joke. "Oh, Miss Merriam spoke before she thought, I guess. What would she do in the city with you?"

Bobby almost lost his breath. "Oh, Dad," he pleaded. "Could I?"

"Now, now, son, you *know* . . ." Chris said patiently. "Maybe next year, you and I. . . ."

"Yeah," Bobby said, "I know . . . but couldn't I?"

Waiting for the train in town, Helen Merriam tried not to examine this new situation. She had done something on impulse, like the others. She didn't want to turn up anything that might be hasty or foolish in it.

It was different getting on the train with Bobby than it had been getting on the train alone. The Christmas look on the other faces no longer islanded her. She felt included and warm. Like the way she'd felt when Chris had brought him and his suitcase to her boardinghouse that morning, explaining to her about his clothes and entrusting his spending money to her.

The train was crowded. She searched for a double seat, but there was none vacant. Then a woman looked up at her and smiled.

"Sit beside me," the woman said. "And your little boy back there. I'm getting off next stop . . . and then you can sit together."

"Oh, thank you," Helen said. "Would you do that, Bobby?"

"Sure," he said. To agree with even the simplest suggestion seemed to give him a brimming pleasure today.

A sudden ridiculous relief went over her that he hadn't added, "Miss Merriam." She'd had the strangest feeling when the woman said, "your little boy": then there wasn't anything about her looks to tell another woman such a thing would not be credible. She felt as if some vague disfigurement had all at once been sloughed off. She'd explain to the woman in a minute, but. . . .

The woman began immediately to talk about her own children. "I have a little boy about the size of yours," she said. "How old is *he*?"

"Nine," Helen said.

Now was the time to explain. The woman would slip away a little, instinctively. This only basis of immediate contact (she'd seen it in so many other women talking to each other about their children) would be severed at once. She hesitated.

"But he takes size eleven in everything," she said.

The woman laughed. "I know," she said. "Don't they grow? I suppose he's all excited about Christmas." She half-sighed. "Well, these are their best years, aren't they?"

Their best years. It gave her a sudden pang. Were what should be his best years slipping by, without his ever knowing what a child's best years, in a full family, should be like? Sitting alone, he had on that look of indifference. She felt like reaching back to touch him.

But sitting with her, later, he was exuberant as any child, with the spell of going somewhere strange and new.

And Helen Merriam herself practised a deceit she wouldn't have believed herself capable of. She deliberately fostered the impression now, of being an ordinary woman travelling at Christmas with her son. To be thought like the others, if only for a few hours, if only with people she would never see again. . . . She even pretended apathy at some of his eager questions about the country they passed through, to make the illusion more convincing.

"Miss Merriam?" he began at once.

"Who's she?" she said quickly, making a show of mock ignorance. "Let's not mention her name till school starts again, eh? We're on a holiday." She winked at him. He didn't understand, but he nodded and gave her back a willing conspiratorial grin.

About the time the lights came on in the train, she thought his face looked strained. He seemed restless. He kept asking, "How much longer before we get there?" She felt a flick of dismay. Was the trip wearing thin already?

Then it came to her. (And with it the thought of all the other times a lonely child might have suffered desperately rather than ask an embarrassing question.)

89

"Watch where that man goes," she whispered. "When he comes out, you better. . . ."

His fearsome gamut over, Bobby's smile was almost triumphant as he came back down the aisle. "Gosh," he said, "this is a swell train, isn't it? I wish it could be Christmas like this all the time, don't you?"

In spite of himself he fell asleep soon after. And riding along in the lighted train, she was so safe in happiness that for the first time she was able to pronounce in her mind the shameful word "alone." She thought: even if it's only a child, and he asleep, it's not like riding in a lighted train alone.

Showing Bobby the city was wonderful: she had something to communicate to someone else. He was fascinated with everything. And though it gave her an ache, it was a kind of precious one, to see him looking at the price tags in the stores and then surreptitiously examining the contents of his purse; to see the look of studied indifference when he was impressed by something, but not wanting to appear strange.

The second morning, the day of Christmas Eve, she was going out to buy herself a new dress.

"You didn't lose the earrings, did you?" Bobby said, coming into her room. "They were in such a little box."

She knew he was disappointed that she hadn't worn them. This was a hint to put them on. Well, they wouldn't look outrageous in the city . . . where half the people wore things that didn't suit them.

"Oh, no," she laughed, "they're safe enough. And I think now's a good time to try them out, eh?"

She took them from her suitcase and fastened them on. Then she went to the mirror, thinking she'd cover them as much as possible with her hair.

But it was funny. There is a certain type of plain appearance which a single bizarre touch—of lipstick, or ornament, or coiffure, or whatever—seems to lift right up into the remarkable. The earrings did that for Miss Mirriam's face. She was astonished. She felt a sudden confidence, a strange buoyancy.

It was funny too about the salesgirls. Before, they'd always shown her matronly dresses. Now they brought out simple but stylish ones. And it was funny that this was the kind of dress she bought. Before she'd always got one which, after it was no longer "good," she could take for school. Now she bought one she couldn't possibly wear in the schoolroom.

She bought a new coat as well; and when the girl asked if she'd take them with her or have them sent, she said, no, she'd wear them. Her old clothes, which the girl packed into a box, looked suddenly like someone else's.

She was really gay that afternoon, as she planned what they'd do Christmas Eve. Would he like to go to a big restaurant for supper, and then to a show? Or would he . . . ?

But Bobby seemed distracted. "If *you* would," was all he'd say. He'd put on an eager face while she was looking at him; but as soon as her glance shifted away, his face would fall into that unassailable preoccupation a child has when he is secretly disturbed. She began to feel baffled.

"Miss Merriam," he said at last (forgetting their compact), "I don't think I feel so good."

Oh, heavens!

"Where, dear?" she said. "How? Are you hot? Let me see."

She put her hand on his forehead. It was cool as ice.

"I think maybe it's in my stomach."

"Where?" she said. "Here? (Appendicitis!) Does it pain?"

"No," he said. "It don't pain. It's just kind of. . . ."

She went quickly to the phone.

"You lie down on your bed," she said (and thought, as she spoke, how that look of indifference had grown on his face last night when it came time to undress—until she'd made an excuse out of his room), "and I'll call a doctor."

"Oh no," he pleaded quickly. "I think maybe it's a little better now." He hesitated a minute. "I think Dad would know what to do."

Her fingers relaxed on the phone. And suddenly she felt a little sick herself.

"Would you like to go back on today's train?" she said.

He had a hard job to maintain the solemn visage of illness long enough that the smile wouldn't take over too suspiciously soon.

"I'm having an awful good time, Miss Merriam," he said earnestly, "but I guess we'd better. Besides, Dad might be kinda lonesome."

She couldn't believe that this was the same train of two days ago.

She felt the old exclusion. She couldn't forget how the excitement of Bobby's trip had turned to ashes when he thought of being away from his father on Christmas Eve. She might be an *ordinary* day's distraction. She wasn't a Christmas Eve thing. He'd left her the way a child you've been amusing leaves you so cruelly completely when another child appears.

She hadn't had time to wrap the packages they'd bought. She had planned that they'd carry some of them in their arms on the way home tomorrow as a badge of belonging. Now, this almost professional talent of hers to make a Christmas package look gay seemed like a fussy, marking, shameful one. She wished her fingers were clumsy and haphazard like most other women's.

The lights came on in the train. They shone out onto the great-flaked Christmas Eve snow which had just begun its hushed expectant falling. She felt the old dread. If it were only twelve o'clock. . . .

When they neared their station she noticed the curious light in the faces of other people who were gathering their luggage together, to get off: the special sight which comes to faces once a year; when you can almost see how they looked when they were children, and what kind of children they were. Her face didn't change.

There'd be no one waiting on the platform: glancing, glancing, and then, with recognition, the face-light flaring up suddenly as if the eyes had leapt a physical barrier. She made no pretence that she and Bobby were mother and son now. What she'd done before, now seemed like an indescribably foolish and shameful thing.

But they *were* met. Chris Fairfield was almost the first person she saw. Rather than the light of greeting, though, there was puzzlement on all their faces.

They moved toward each other through the jostling crowd. I suppose that woman would assume this was my husband, she thought. But wincing now, and wishing she could be somewhere alone, out of sight.

"Well!" Chris exclaimed. "What happened?"

"Hi, Dad," Bobby said.

"Bobby didn't feel very well," she said, letting her tone of voice tell the true story. "He thought you'd know what to do."

"Ohhhhh." He tilted his head backward and pursed his lips. "I see. But that broke up your trip too. That's a shame."

"You've got a new suit and coat," Bobby said quickly. Chris had. He looked almost boyish in them.

"Yeah," he said. "Y'know what? I took it into my head to go in on the evening train and surprise you tomorrow morning."

For a second he looked a little crestfallen. Like Bobby, she thought, when he was disappointed about something, never dreaming that the disappointment was showing on his face. And she thought too: he couldn't bear to have me share Bobby's Christmas entirely . . . not even once.

"Miss Merriam's got new clothes too," Bobby said, still trying to head off any discussion of his guilt.

"So I see," Chris said. He laughed. "Well, it looks like we're all dressed up and no place to go."

She'd never seen him in a jocular mood like this. It must be the new clothes, she thought. He looked like she'd felt when she first put on the earrings and looked into the mirror.

"*I* know," Bobby said eagerly. "Seeing you planned to go anyway, why don't we *all* go back on the evening train?"

Chris glanced at Miss Merriam.

"Oh no, Bobby," she said. "We couldn't do that. Now we're here."

The old awkwardness had come back to her more acutely than ever. His father's idea to surprise Bobby on Christmas morning would have been fine for Bobby, but she'd have felt like a stranger. She was thankful that Bobby had brought her home.

"Well," Chris said. "I guess . . . if we're going home . . . we better pick up a car before they're all spoken for." He moved off.

She didn't know why that should have anything to do with it, but watching him back-to, dressed up for town but not quite as glib and pushing as the others, his nature somehow crystalized and clarified by the presence of strangers, she realized something for the first time.

I love him, she thought. She had the crazy, following, thought: if it hadn't been for my new clothes and his new suit and meeting here in this strange place, I'd never have known it. She knew too why she loved this child so particularly. It was primarily as an extension of his father. The whole picture came to her so quickly she felt faint. She felt like an old woman, glimpsing a vision of some other way it might have been if she'd only known . . . way back then.

Chris signalled for them. He collected the suitcases and they were ready to go. It was a car with no trunk.

"You two set in back with the suitcases and your son in front?" the driver said.

She winced again. Would people never stop making that mistake? It seemed now as if the whole world were in some conspiracy to mock her. She glanced at Chris. He was half-smiling, as if the man's implication were such a ridiculous idea he couldn't keep his face straight. He doesn't even take the trouble to correct it, she thought.

"I'll sit in front," she said.

"Aw no," Bobby said. "Let's all sit in behind, together. We can make room."

It was exactly the kind of Christmas Eve you saw on all the cards. Calm unhurried moonlight fell on the white road, polishing the sled-runner tracks like isinglass, except where the dark shadows of the spruces latticed them. The cold star-fire seemed softened, and flakes of snow drifted down dreamily against the headlights, like leaves from a twig. Even the car seemed to lose its machine-coldness. Its purr sounded cosy and animate. She saw the night with the awful clarity a night has for you, if your feelings are not attuned to it. We're part of the picture on the cards too, she thought ironically: a man and a woman riding home and the child between them falling asleep in spite of himself.

The car radio was playing "Holy Night."

"Maybe you're sick of the carols," the driver said.

"Well, I think they overdo them, don't you?" she said, as casually as she could manage. He turned the radio off.

When they'd almost reached her boardinghouse, she glanced at her watch. It was only half-past ten. She caught her breath. An hour and a half yet. . . .

And now Chris would *have* to explain to the driver, when he let her out. They'd probably joke about it after she'd gone up the path, the mood he was in tonight.

Opposite the driveway, when he still gave no sign to the driver, she sat up in the seat. But Chris shook his head.

"We might as well just make the one stop," he whispered. "It's only a jump. I'll walk back with you. And I got something I made at the house I want to show you."

She relaxed in the seat again, but she couldn't summon interest in even Bobby's Christmas things now.

At the house the driver had no change for the ten-dollar bill Chris gave him. They both examined the contents of all their pockets in the light of the head lamps, but they still couldn't make it.

She looked in her purse. "I have some change," she said; and among them they worked the thing out. She had seen a man and woman doing *that* before too.

Bobby didn't awake when Chris took him out of the car. He carried him to the house in his arms.

"I guess you'll have to open the door," he said to her. "The key's in my outside pocket there."

She fished out the key, her fingers almost useless with self-consciousness, and opened the door.

"Perhaps I'd better take him right up and put him in bed, do you think?" he said. "You can light the lamp. I guess the big one's in the front room. The matches are there by the dish cupboard. I'll be just a minute. Then I'll walk back with you."

She lit the lamp. There was no fire in the room stove, but the tree sprang awake at the light, and its soft incarnate smell warmed the air.

Chris seemed to have lost most of his earlier sureness and jocularity when he came downstairs again; to be more his old awkward self. He was carrying something in his hand. Though the object wasn't wrapped, she couldn't imagine what it was until he passed it to her.

"It's for you," he said abruptly. She thought of Bobby with the earrings.

She gazed at it, speechless. It was the loveliest thing she had ever seen . . . but she couldn't very well say that. Because it was a little statuette of herself.

She could see that it was nothing he'd made in the last few days; he must have been working on it, carving and tinting, for weeks. Sometime or other he must have studied every detail of her face, to repeat them. And yet—the wonderful part—he hadn't repeated them exactly. It didn't repeat the tidy way she looked; somehow, its intricate perfection caught the fluid, flexible, outgoing way she felt inside. And the dress wasn't like any he'd ever seen her wear. It was a dress more like the one she had just bought. And in the ears, in absolutely clear and perfect detail, were replicas of the very earrings, the extravagant earrings she was wearing now.

She couldn't think what to say. He had turned aside. She thought of Bobby at the blackboard.

"So *you* chose the earrings?" she said.

"Well, it was his idea," he said. "I picked them out."

The breath he drew was so deep it was audible. "You should have a ring to go with them," he added.

She didn't pretend she didn't know what he meant.

But curiously, right then, she felt the exclusion more acutely even than in the train. It's for Bobby, she thought. He saw how well it went with the three of us at the tree the other afternoon. He knows that Bobby needs a woman in the house. I love him and he's asking me to marry him; but why, when it comes my way, does even this have to be a cold-blooded, reasoned thing . . . in connection with someone else?

When she didn't answer, he spoke again. Almost doggedly now; as if once he'd started it must all come out.

"I know it's asking a lot," he said. "There'd be Bobby to look after. And maybe Bobby . . . I don't know. But he likes you, you know that. And well, maybe even if he *was* jealous of you for a little while . . . well, if you would . . . a man has to think of his own life a little too, I guess."

He looked up.

Now what did I say *then*, he thought, to make her face change like that?

He had no way of knowing that even before the full effect struck her of realizing that it was for herself alone . . . that so far from being in connection with Bobby entirely, even if Bobby should be *difficult* for awhile, he'd still . . . that someone, he, *had* been hinting to spend Christmas with her—that even before that, she was thinking: never again will I have my cards mailed on time. That she was thinking: never again can the others ask me somewhere without having to consider the possibility of me having another plan. That she couldn't speak because she had just glanced at her watch, and it was only half-past eleven, and she wasn't afraid at all.

When she laughed, she looked like the statuette, physically.

"But can you afford a ring," she said, "after what the earrings cost you?"

"What?" His face was comically irresolute between amusement and embarrassment. "Did Bobby stick that slip in the box? Well, the little. . . ."

Then he chuckled, and she felt the earrings in her ears like Christmas stars. This was really like it was when she had seen a quiet man and a quiet woman, who were nothing more than just quiet people in other's eyes, chuckling together in the sharing of an understanding and humour that was like no one else's . . . at some action of a child. Or at anything whatever.

"But listen to me, Helen," he said, "what about the ring? You haven't said about the ring."

She nodded. "Yes," she said quietly. "But we'd better go now."

She was thinking that if they hurried there'd still be time for her to turn on the radio in her room and catch one last carol anyway.

Last Delivery
Before Christmas

My father had been dead two years, and that August my mother married again. She married Syd Weston. It was that circumstance which. . . . But you would have to understand quite thoroughly about Mother and Syd and me to have any of that following Christmas make sense.

For Mother's sake I tried not to let resentment of my stepfather show. But a child of ten doesn't have the technique for that kind of acting. *I* didn't, anyway. I remember how angry I used to get with my face sometimes. Other people's faces could keep a secret for them. But whenever I'd glimpse mine in any reflecting surface it seemed to be tattling everything that went on behind it.

I suppose I got that from my father. Though with a crucial difference. His face used to be right out with everything, too, but in an expansive entirely unselfconscious way. I believe, if you'd asked him to describe his face, he'd have had to *think* a minute to know what it really looked like. (Where had that outward look gone, I wondered, the day they took me in to look at him, with the flower smell like a silence gone sickly in the parlour, and the yellower sections of the drawn-down blinds like the first hint of a mortality even in the green fields outside?)

He never turned things over in his mind as I did. I suppose I got that from Mother. I have that curse of sensing immediately the degree of discordance among any group I enter—with a sort of responsibility, as if the guilt for it were my own. Mother had that too.

That's why most of the time I tried to hide from her how Syd and I jarred. Syd's face hardly told on him at all. It just seemed to listen.

Syd was no stranger. His small tidy farm was right next to ours. There wasn't even a fence along the line between us. I remember that when Father would mow there first the swath would go across the line and back, crooked as a ram's horn; but when Syd made the first cut his swath would be straight as a die, just inside the line on his part.

The only time I had ever seen Syd's face give him away was the day of my father's funeral. Heartbroken though I was that day I studied everyone's face, as any child will, to see how they were feeling and to see what kind of look each of them was giving me. A simulated grief sat on the other faces like a kind of demureness but Syd's face had such a look it startled me right out of myself. It had a sort of desperate, waking-in-a-strange-place look, especially when he glanced at Mother.

He would never come into our house after that. But how many times, it seemed by accident, he would be working alongside the road when I went by and ask me how we were making out. And it got so I went over to his place quite a bit. He would let me take the reins of the team until we came to a ditch or had to cross the main road, and let me pick out small rocks to chink the well with, in a way that made me feel as if I were grown-up and doing a man's work. I remember how I'd spit sideways when both my hands were busy, the way men do.

I never felt any constraint with him then—unless some of the other kids came by; then I'd make some excuse to leave immediately. Because, among ourselves, we called him "old man Weston." Not because he was old or cranky, but because he lived alone. And no one is as cruelly ostracized by kids as someone a little "different."

I remember one day I said to him, "Syd, why didn't you ever get married?" It used to be a gig of mine to try to startle people with odd questions like that. But Syd's face didn't alter a bit.

"Well now, I don't know," he said.

"Y'know, Syd," I said, "you look real good when you're dressed up and Mum said you used to be the best dancer she ever danced with!"

"Did she now!" he said. His face didn't change then either, but he brushed away the shavings from the auger hole he was boring, with a sudden little movement that reminded me somehow of the way a dust devil will catch at a neat windrow of hay and disarrange it.

He never talked about Mother directly. But occasionally when I would do or say something that I couldn't see was any way different from the way anyone else would do or say it, he would murmur: "Ain't that Laura for you!" Laura was my mother.

I knew, of course, that Syd had gone with Mother when they were both young, from hearing the women joke her about it sometimes. "Do you mind how we used to cross out Syd Weston's name with yours in school and they'd both come out 'marriage'?" or "Is it true that Syd was hangin' off till he had a hundred dollars in the bank?"

And I knew how Jess Matthews (that was my father) had come here to Westfield with a lumbering crew and married her within a month. It was a sort of local legend how that night at the pie social when he did the tricks (he could do tricks that *no* one could see through) he got Mother to come up and hold out her left hand and, after exhibiting his own empty palms and rolling up his sleeves, made a quick magician's gesture in the air and before she knew it there was an engagement ring on her finger, and she standing there looking as if she didn't know whether she wanted to laugh or cry.

Father was always laughing, or ready to laugh. He'd pay the fiddler as much as five dollars to play an extra hour at the Friday-night dances in the schoolhouse; and there was always a bunch of kids hanging around him. He could turn out to have completely forgotten something he'd promised you, something you'd counted on for days; and then with just some conspiratorial little nudge or wink become as infallible as ever, and make you feel as big and wonderful as he was.

I mentioned that pie social affair to Mother one time. "Was Syd there that night?" I asked.

"No," she said. "He had to haul in grain. He said, 'It looks like rain, and if that load of oats gets wet again tonight it won't be good for anything.'"

That'd be Syd all right. And then I thought: wasn't it funny that anyone would recall the words—the exact words—someone else had said about a little thing like that so long ago?

Syd never came inside our house again until that August evening. He'd give us a load of wood now and then, but he'd haul it into the dooryard some afternoon Mother was away. And she'd send *me* to thank him and try to make him take pay for it. And whenever Mother would bring out a plate of cake and a jug of lemonade to the men in the afternoon, Syd always seemed to be off in a corner some place, clipping around a rock (every haying season Father planned to blast the big rocks in the field that fall, but somehow he never got it done) with the hand scythe.

I can still remember that August evening. I remember how peculiarly still it was. I had gone to bed before dark, so I could run off all by myself, like a reel in my head, the excitement of going away. Mother had finally made up her mind.

From my bed by the window I could see Syd sitting on the front doorstep of his small house. To a child the idea of oneself going away makes sober rooted people seem almost incredible, unbelievably stupid. You feel that somehow someone should make them *understand*.

The stillness didn't bother me but I know now the kind of stillness it was for the older ones. It was one of those nights of drought when the slamming of a screen door or the tapping of a neighbour's hammer sounds astonishingly near. And yet everything else seems untouchably far away. There is only the fitful pulse of the blind against the screen where you sit, hearing only your mind not-think.

I saw Mother go outside. She walked along the edge of the flower bed, picking off a wilted nasturtium leaf here and there, or straightening the sticks beside the rosebushes. But she did these things inertly, as you do things on a day you are trying to whittle away with movement—a day when it seems as if each time you look at the clock more time must have passed than the clock has counted.

I knew Mother wasn't happy, like me, about going away. But what could she do? A farm can go on for a few years without a man's steady care, but what can a woman do when the ditches in the low parts grass over and fill in, and the shingles blow up on the very top of the barn roof, and the time comes when all the fence wire is rusted too brittle even to splice? Even if she could pay to have these things fixed, what about the night when the gale blows the big shed doors open, or the day the cow is choking on an apple and no one within sound of your call?

It was coming dusk when I saw Alf Steele walking up the road. He stopped for a minute opposite Syd's. Their voices came to me clear as voices over water.

"Ain't ya comin' to school meetin', Syd?" Alf called.

"I guess not," Syd answered. "Not tonight."

"No? Well. . . ." And then, just before resuming his pace, Alf added, "Did ya know Laura's goin' away? Anyhow, that's the talk."

"Goin' away?" Syd said. "No. Where?"

"They say her brother Frank's got her a job in the city. Montreal, ain't it, Frank is?"

Syd came to his feet so quickly I thought he was going out to the road to question Alf further. But he didn't. He turned abruptly and went inside the house.

It couldn't have been more than fifteen minutes later that I heard our screen door open and close.

"Why, Syd!" Mother exclaimed. The heat hole over the kitchen stove was right beside my bed, and I could catch everything that was said below.

"I can't set down," Syd blurted out. "I just came over to. . . ."

I knew he did sit down though. In my mind I could picture him snapping the crown of his cap to the peak and unsnapping it. And I could see Mother taking off her apron and smoothing out the wrinkles in her skirt. I could see her place a smile on her face, consciously. It wouldn't be a false smile, but it wouldn't hide her feelings half as thoroughly as she believed.

"Laura," Syd said—and the words came out propulsively, as if they were a stoppage in his throat—"you ain't goin' away, are you?"

I could see the precarious smile drop off Mother's face. "I don't know, Syd," she said. Her voice sounded freer, now that her thought and her speech need not keep to separate channels. "I guess so. I don't know what to do. I can't seem to think. Frank wants me to go out there with him. I wouldn't like the city, I know, but things here have got to the point where. . . ." She would be sitting there ironing one arm with the palm of her other hand.

There was quite a long silence. And then I heard Syd say,

"Don't, Laura . . . don't. . . . " I knew what had happened. I always hated to see Mother cry. She'd draw in a deep breath and hold it hard, as if against the muscles of her face. But then the muscles would begin to give way, one group after another. And her mouth would look as if it hurt her, physically.

"I guess I'm making a fool of myself," Mother said, all at once contrite. "Do you remember what you used to say: 'I never saw how crying over anything ever helped'?"

I heard a chair scrape out then. Syd would be standing there, clumsy with the thought of his hand lying on her shoulder and equally clumsy with the thought of taking it away, because it seemed to help her, touched for a moment by that curious glow you feel when someone puts a particular memory of you into words, when you had feared that nothing more than a general memory of you might exist in anyone anywhere.

"Laura," he said suddenly, "*don't* go 'way. Why couldn't you and me . . . ?" I think she looked up, surprised and not surprised. And then he spoke almost with savagery. "I ain't the old—" he couldn't seem to find the word which should come next, "—people think I am. I got feelin's too."

I had a moment of consternation. It sounded as if Syd hated the way he was. All people in any way strange—it had never occurred to me that they might have to go on being that way because other people kept expecting it of them.

And then I covered my head with the bedclothes, not to hear any more. I knew we would not be going away now.

But even that was crowded out of my mind. I had only one bitter, burning thought. You needn't be openly rebellious against a usurper, but if you observed forever one little obstinacy known only to yourself, your original loyalty would still be intact. For Mother's sake I wouldn't make any fuss. But I would go right on calling him "Syd." I would never, *never*, call him "Dad."

I think that at the beginning Mother didn't really worry at all about me keeping Syd at arm's length. It was to be expected. But in a few weeks, when the situation hadn't changed, a constraint fell over all of us. This constraint was not continuous, of course—three people cannot live together in the country without being unreservedly fused most of the time by little excitements, little catastrophes, and the news brought in by one or the other from outside. But I had the child's talent for that most punishing rebuke: of withdrawing a little, as if behind an invisible boundary, just when the other has begun to think your estrangement must have been something he imagined.

Syd would show me how to mow, placing my hands just so on the scythe and I trying to hold them right there; and then, following my swath, he'd say, "That's right, that's right, you got the hang of it," and I'd say, "I guess you can finish it," and go hang up the scythe in the crotch of a tree. Or we might be preparing to go raspberrying in the back burntland, searching about for the water jug, gathering the tins, checking in the lunch basket to see if the salt and pepper for the eggs hadn't been forgotten, and I'd turn to Mother and say, "Is *he* going to stay all day with us?"

It was then that Mother's face would get that awful look: resignation, but resignation worse for never being safe from a hope perpetually renewed and as perpetually struck down. She would sometimes pass her hand over her forehead vaguely as if there were some possible kind of motion that would wipe this film over things away. And for a while after that it would seem as if everything Syd and I said (or didn't say) to each other would sound sort of loud.

The situation was never openly admitted, and at first Mother tried to overcome it. If I let slip something spontaneous like, "I'd like to see Syd on that mowin' machine o' Reg's. I bet he could mow that field in two hours!" she'd seize upon my remark and repeat it to him ever so casually. Or if Syd were to say, "Why, that kid can sow grass seed as good as a man—better'n *some* men!" she'd repeat that to me. But her casualness was so transparent (each of us knew what the situation was) that her ruses turned out to be only embarrassing. And after a little she gave them up.

Otherwise, things certainly went smoother with us than they had ever done when Father was alive. There was always dry wood in the shed, the water pails were always full, the clothes line was now spliced so strong it never let Mother's clean sheets down into the mud, and . . . well, that precarious bridge from one day to the next seemed to be completely shored up.

But how could a child love anyone for that kind of thing? How could that kind of thoughtfulness take the place of the knack Father had of immediately winning you over to his way of seeing that serious concern over *any*thing belonged way down below fun?

It was queer about that, though. Once Mother lost the new

scissors she'd spent the last cent in her purse for. "Now where could I have laid them?" she said, frowning with worry. "Did you have 'em openin' the flour bag?" Father asked. "No." "Didn't have 'em out clippin' flowers?" "No, I had the little scissors out there." He thought. "Sure you didn't have 'em cuttin' up citron for a pound cake?" She had laughed so we'd had to be stern with her to keep her from hysterics. But the minute her laughter had subsided her face looked as worried as before. Now, when she laughed with Syd about anything—though less often and not half as hysterically—an echo of the laughter would stay on in her eyes long after the laughter itself was done.

If only half-consciously, I resented that. I would think: if he'd ever once do something that wasn't so darned sensible, so darned predictable.

It was only when I would actually surprise myself in a moment of accepting Syd wholeheartedly that I was deliberately cruel to him.

I remember one day I was watching him make a birdhouse for me, completely engrossed in the expert way his large hands could manage the miniature splices. I was fingering absently a little gadget that hung from the buttonhole of my jacket. It was a tiny cube of wood, whittled so that only a sphere remained inside its open-faced cage.

He looked up. "Ronnie," he said, "one o' them edges there is way longer than the others. Let me square her up for you."

I bridled. "Naw," I said, "don't bother. That's all right."

"It won't take but a minute," he said. "Let's see it."

I moved off. "Naw, that's all right," I said. "My father made me that."

He didn't say a word.

Another day a cattle buyer was looking at the oxen. I felt just like a third man with him and Syd. Syd never said anything like, "Now keep friggin' with that sprayer till ya break it!" or "Look outa the man's way there," the way other men (even Father) did, to cut down kids in the barn.

"You oughta seen the rock that team hauled off last week!" I said.

The buyer grinned at me. "That's quite a boy you got there, Mr. Weston," he said, in a hearty salesman's voice. "I guess he's gonna be as good a judge o' cattle as his old man, eh?"

"He's not my old man," I said. "My father is dead."

I was glad Mother didn't see Syd's face then. Come to think of it, perhaps it used to give him away more often than I've made it sound.

I think the fortnight before Christmas must have been the worst of all for Mother. She was very happy because we had more money for the mail order that year than ever before, and I knew she kept waiting for me to study the catalogue, so that she could glimpse which page I kept it open at longest. But I acted as if Christmas didn't matter to me in the least. Other years I used to nag and nag at her to get the order off early. But that year it was she herself who had to say: "My soul, this is the fifteenth. We better get that order off this very night or it'll be too late."

The night when we used to clear off the dining-room table and get out all the writing paraphernalia, pretending we were ordering each other's gifts from one page in the catalogue, while a finger was holding it open, secretly, to another; with her putting down the things for me and then folding the order sheet over her writing until I had put her gifts below; and making a solemn promise that when she added up the total she wouldn't even glance at anything but the figures—that night used to be almost as exciting as Christmas itself.

But that year I let her sit at the table alone. It gave me an almost sickening pang to see her there, taking as long as ever to select those things for me which would be useful but still have something of the "present" quality about them, and sobered (but so unprotestingly) by my withholding of connivance in the spirit of the occasion thus made so desolate for her to support alone. But I couldn't help it. I didn't even pretend to glance at the numbers of the pages she was copying from.

Once she said, so extra casually I knew it had come on her tongue and then faltered a good many times before she could speak it: "Would you like to put something down for your father?" Syd was outside.

I knew it would have delighted her beyond anything if I'd answered something like, "Yeah. What could I get him?—something that would really surprise him!" But what I said was, "No, I guess not. It'd be kinda foolish gettin' him something with his own money."

I didn't put anything down for him or, because it would be paid for with his money, for her either. Syd himself had never once enquired what I wanted. If he had, I was prepared to say, "Oh, anything. I don't care," with deliberate indifference. But just the same I almost hated him for not asking.

Syd took the letter to the post office the next morning. Any letter that needed a money order fixed up for enclosure Mother usually took. But he offered specially (almost insisted) to take this one. For a moment I wondered if he wanted to look at the sheet to see if there was anything on it for him (and for a moment I had another pang: to think of this little curiosity being rewarded by the sight of nothing more exciting than a work shirt). But then I knew that spying wasn't like Syd. This would be just like any other letter, to him, I thought.

Times before, the day the Christmas order had finally gone off had been one of the wonderful ones. It had seemed as if we'd set in motion some benevolent mechanism which would be busy contriving something splendid for us all through the following days, even when we were not thinking about it. But that morning, this mood of indifference I had chosen spoiled everything.

About ten o'clock, Mother's hand froze suddenly on the pump handle. "Oh, dear!" she said. "I forgot to put down the tissue paper and seals. Now isn't that . . . ?"

She looked at me appealingly. I thought, if I'd only helped her (though the bitter regret which the "only" implied was disowned almost as soon as I recognized it). *I* wouldn't have forgotten. But I didn't say a word. And after that, Mother suddenly gave up trying to encourage my Christmas spirit.

It is curious how a child will prolong a sort of sulkiness that has started as whim until it hardens into obstinacy, resisting every effort to dislodge him from it; and how the most dismaying thing of all is when the others at last take his mood at its face value and leave him entirely alone.

I was, however, to know a dismay even worse before the next week was out.

Christmas was on Saturday of that week, and the order should come on the Tuesday or Wednesday before. But it didn't come Tuesday—or Wednesday. And when I went to the post office on Thursday, certain that it would be there (and thankful by this time that the excitement of the package arriving could save my face by seeming to sweep me out of my mood, rather than my having to abandon it of my own free will), the package was not there either. There was just a card, saying it had gone to the station. Whenever you have deliberately chosen to be perverse, it seems that everything else is quick to fall into line.

"Now what did they send it by express for?" Mother said. "I can't think of anything heavy in it."

"It's cheaper that way," Syd said.

"I know," Mother said. "But Christmas time . . . when everyone's in such a rush. . . ."

"We can give the card to Cliff tomorrow," Syd said—Cliff was the mailman—"and he'll go to the station and get it for us."

"Why, yes," Mother said. "I never thought of that. Cliff'll get it. He's a good soul."

I was so relieved I nearly cried.

That night the snow came. When Syd came in from his late trip to the barn he stood in the porch almost solid white, with his arms angled out from his sides for someone to brush him off with the broom. "Why, Syd!" Mother cried, "Is it snowing?—like *that*?" And after I'd gone up to bed I kept my lamp lit for a little while to watch the great flakes float and eddy down past the window pane, like an infinite fragmentation of some beautiful white healing silence. Snow for Christmas.

But with it, while I slept, the wind came.

And when I looked out the window in the morning the whole world seemed buried in a great sea of snow: huge, billowing, porpoise-backed waves of it, caught up around the corners of the buildings into long breaker tips that reached almost to the eaves. I saw Syd starting to shovel a tunnel to the barn. He didn't bend, but reached, at the drift before him. Here and there a spot of road would show bare as your hand in a trough of the waves, but on either side of the spot you couldn't even guess where the road went. I looked again at Syd's tunnel. He had scraped it right down to the grass, but I saw that already the wind had sifted enough snow back into it that a deep track could be made.

I knew that the men would not break out the roads until the wind had died down completely. Not till afternoon, anyway. I knew the mail would not go today. And this was the last day before Christmas. And so the order would never get here for Christmas at all.

I thought, for a second, how I had almost believed in my indifference to Christmas a couple of weeks ago. How could that have been possible? Was this storm, like the order going to the station, some sort of punishment? Perhaps the mere focusing of memory on it tends to exaggerate a past despair. But it seems to me that those moments when I stood there at the window, realizing for the first time that the unthinkable *could* happen, may well have been the bleakest of my whole life.

Mother tried her best to console me. She said we had the tree, anyway (Syd had got that a couple of days ago, an absolutely perfect one), and we had lots of candy and nuts, and, well, the things would only be a little late. I could hardly keep from shouting when I answered, "What good are things *after* Christmas?" Especially with no tissue paper to wrap them in, and the time already past before which they must not be opened. It would be just like an order you'd sent in the summertime.

Syd didn't say a word. He didn't seem to be disturbed at all. And later in the morning, when I stood in the porch door, praying that by some last-minute miracle I'd see the ox teams come breaking the roads and the mailman's horse behind them (though the wind was blowing stronger now, rather than less), I heard Mother say to him almost frantically: "Syd, what could we fix up for Ronnie? We've just got to have something for him."

He said, "I don't know. What could we fix up for him?" But he didn't sound really concerned—in the next breath he asked her if she could get dinner early. I couldn't see what difference it made when we ate, or if we ate at all, with the whole long empty day ahead.

After an early dinner, we started to trim the tree. Mother and I. Syd got out his rifle and took it apart to clean it.

I helped Mother as conscientiously as I had ever done, because I was too desolate even to be sullen. But I worked with that awful docility with which you put on your best clothes as carefully as ever though the occasion is a farewell at the train, maybe for the last time. And then a shaft of how it might have been—trimming the tree on this cloistering day (the wind was shriller now), with the contents of the order hidden no more secretly than beneath the sofa and, because of that, my pledge not to look all the more torturingly sweet—would pierce me right to the bone.

About one o'clock, Syd came into the parlour. "I think I'll take a scout around with the gun," he said. So that's why he'd wanted an early dinner.

"Syd," Mother exclaimed, "you're not going hunting, a day like this?"

"It's a good day for huntin'," he said. "The wind'd be just about right in the spruce, and the snowshoein' ain't bad."

In one direction from our house was the road to town and in the other, across some narrow fields, was the dense woods. Twenty solid miles of it.

"Well . . ." Mother said resignedly. "But now you watch out a tree doesn't fall on you or something."

I was so shocked that Syd could leave us alone on this day that I didn't even resent it. I just watched him go across the field, lost in and then appearing out of the spasmodic gusts of wind-driven snow as if he were evaporating and then solidifying again.

We didn't pay much attention to the storm until we had finished working on the tree. In the morning the wind had blown hard, but unconcernedly. Now it was getting rough. Not vicious yet, but rough.

"I wonder if he took his compass," Mother said suddenly. She went to the pantry. The compass was still hanging on its nail. I knew you couldn't lose Syd if you tried—but just the same I was half-annoyed at her for checking up on the compass. It would have been more comfortable not to have known he didn't have it.

About three o'clock the wind became really vicious, like an animal become ravening with the taste of its own violence. The air looked like one of those blizzards that sheep on an old calendar are seen huddling against. The trees bent and writhed constantly and the wind howled at the corners of the house as it sucked itself wildly across the fields.

And now, as if out of some place wrenched open by the wind, the cold came; depositing its sharp knives on the panes.

As the afternoon wore on, the uneasiness in both of us grew to active worry. But neither of us mentioned it. Partly as if by not naming it you could achieve protection, however flimsy, from the thing you feared, and partly because it had become so difficult for us to discuss Syd at all, let alone a mutual concern for him.

We tried to fake an interest in small tasks. But the instant there'd be a slight lull in the storm, one or the other would immediately say, "I believe it's lettin' up," or "Of course, inside it always looks worse than it is." The next instant a redoubled clap of wind would make the chimney gasp as if the very breath of the house were being sucked outside, to be spun about, captured and lost forever, and our automatic glances at each other would seem to collide with almost physical effect—as glances do when smoke is discovered curling out from some place where no smoke should be.

And then we began one at a time to make excuses, peering out the frosted window toward the woods. The Christmas tree was like a mockery. It was like the guest from another way of life who happens to be staying with you when some private trouble strikes, so that you are denied even a natural as-with-neighbours reaction to it, because of appearance's sake.

It got so the only things of any reality in the whole house seemed to be Syd's unspoken name and the tick of the clock. And it was odd the situations my mind chose to recall him in: always one something like his maybe looking at the order sheet and seeing nothing for him there but the work shirt.

About four, Mother got supper. "Syd'll be hungry," she said, "after the early dinner and tramping in the woods." But I knew that was only an excuse. I knew she had the foolish idea that supper ready would somehow beckon him home.

But supper was ready, and then growing cold on the back of the stove, and still he hadn't come. And then, supper *waiting* made the whole thing more clamorous than ever. It was early, but already there was a hint of darkness coming. As if the wind had broken into the hold of night too, and let dusk loose beforehand.

Just then the clock struck the half-hour. Suddenly Mother leapt up. "He should be home now," she said. "I'm going down to Alf's and see if he thinks we ought to. . . ."

I leapt up too. I felt an inexpressible relief, now that this intolerable pretence of casualness was over.

"I'm goin' with you," I said. I expected her to oppose that, but she didn't. "Well . . . all right," she said.

I got my heavy clothes on first, and went in to look out the parlour window once more—openly, avidly, now. There was nothing but that marching blur and the mourning trees. When she was ready she came in too.

"See any sign of him?" she said.

"No," I said. She looked as if the muscles of her face were starting to break up.

We were just turning from the window when all at once she put her hand on my arm. "Hark!" she said. "Wasn't that the back door?"

We both rushed to the kitchen. And there he was, standing by the door, the snow so driven into his clothes, and his eyebrows and mustache so encrusted with it, that he was hardly recognizable.

"Syd," Mother cried, "Oh Syd. . . ." She ran and put her arms about him and her face against his shoulder, snow and all.

"What's the trouble?" Syd said, startled. "What's wrong?" It had never occurred to him that we'd be worried on his account. He thought something dreadful must have happened to *us*.

"You," Mother cried. "You . . . out in this. We've been almost crazy. Where have you been?" Her questions tumbled over each other before he could get out a single word. "Where did you come from? We didn't see you. We've been watching the woods all afternoon, haven't we, Ronnie? Where's your gun? Were you lost?"

"I didn't come by the woods," Syd said. "I come the road."

"The road? Here, let me shake that jumper off in the woodbox. You'll get your death." (I ran into the pantry for a knife to scrape the icicles off.) "Where's your gun?"

Syd sort of grinned. "In the barn," he said. The barn was way down from the house, in the opposite direction from the woods.

"The *barn*?"

Syd didn't answer. He opened the door and reached back into the porch. I thought he was reaching for the old broom.

When he straightened up, I couldn't believe my eyes. Everyone knows one miracle in his life, and this was mine. For in his hand he carried the Christmas order!

"Syd!" Mother cried. "You've been to town! You lugged that order all the way home!" Then, for a second, plain curiosity displaced her agitation. "Is that *our* order?" she said. "Look at the size of it, and the shape of it. I don't remember. . . ." It was a huge package, obviously containing some long almost unwrappable object at the bottom. No wonder it had gone to the station.

I couldn't say a word. I was inundated by the soft glow of danger past, the Christmas order was right here in the house, the tree had suddenly become an intimate again—and now the wind and the cold and the dark were not enemies anymore: just things that could be let go their way, their violence merely heightening the sense of our own containment.

But it was not so much any of that as something else. It was as if I were seeing in Syd a different man. It wasn't that he had walked six miles to town and back on a day like this to get the order. It was that he had wanted to *surprise* us. It was that he had gone to all that manoeuvre of pretended indifference, of cleaning his gun, of actually going into the woods while we watched, and then cutting back across the field, leaving his gun in the barn, and skirting the pasture till he struck the road to town. It was that, for this effect of surprise, he had done someting that had so little common sense about it, that was so crazy, it was almost childish. . . .

And when he fished way down inside the very last layer of heavy clothing and said, "Didn't you mention somethin' about forgettin' to order the tissue paper and seals," and I knew he had got even them, at some store in town . . . well, I had still another thing to bless them for: for not remarking on my speechlessness, for making their own voices loud enough to cover up the other sound I couldn't help—crying.

Syd brushed the snow from the package and took it into the dining room to unwrap, while Mother was taking up the supper. When she went down the cellar for the creamer he came to the dining-room door and beckoned to me. I went in and he closed the door.

He had put all the parcels under the couch except one. It was on the dining-room table. A bright enamelled case, with the top up and, inside, what I thought must surely be the most gorgeous comb, brush, and mirror set anyone had ever seen.

I gasped. He must have added that at the post office, I thought, the morning he took the order over. He (Syd!) must have asked the postmistress for her catalogue. I almost cried again: to think of what an effort that must have been for him, and of him trying to squeeze the article number and description in the tiny spaces provided, with that big handwriting of his that always looked as if it came so hard. I'd never touched anything with such reverence as the heavy mirror I picked up and then laid back again into its pleated satin socket.

"Think we could wrap it up kinda nice?" Syd said, almost sheepishly.

"Now?" I said. "Right now?"

"Might as well," he said. "Case she goes snoopin'."

It did look nice when we were done. I wouldn't have believed Syd could turn the corners of the flimsy tissue paper so deftly, and hold them so perfectly in line while I put on the very biggest seals in the whole package. We hid it in the sideboard drawer, beneath the tablecloth.

Mother looked up when we came into the kitchen. Her face had that odd blend of caution and hope.

"Now what are you two up to?" she said.

"Ask him," I said, grinning. "Ask Dad."

Maybe I only seem to remember that a swift locking glance passed between them, before they dropped their eyes. But I do know that Mother's face had the most indescribable look on it. As if something had divided her between such perfect joy and such fear that such perfect joy could not last.

But the next morning, with the wind composed and penitent again, and in the lamplight before dawn, when I saw the package beneath the tree that *no* one could wrap—the bright, gleaming, new twenty-two rifle that Syd must have added also at the post office—then, I think, she knew it would last.

"D'ya like it?" Syd said shyly. He didn't touch the twenty-two himself, but he kept standing right near it all the time.

"*Like* it?" I said.

"But, Syd," Mother said, "do you think he's old enough for a gun?"

"Oh, Mother . . . !" I cried.

"Now, stop worryin'!" Syd chided her. "There ain't nothin' about a gun, if anyone's careful."

She still didn't look too happy about it. But I think that, in a funny way, this was the most rewarding thing for her of all: that Syd and I were taking sides against her. With that peculiar sense of omniscience that seems to come only with intense happiness, I thought (as a child thinks such things, recognizing the essence only of words that would express them): now, at last, with the man and the boy disputing with the woman the wisdom of a gun for the boy, we are a family.

And I knew that, though I had no real gift for either of them, somehow I had managed to give them a present better than any to be found in the catalogue.

And I knew too, if I could see it, wherever it was, my father's face would be right in on this with us; and that, if I could hear him, he would be saying: "Now, y'see? What did I tell you about your frettin'? Everything always turns out right."

113

REMEMBRANCE OF THINGS PAST

The Wild Goose

I've never stopped missing my brother Jeff.

I'm all right; and then I pick up the rake he mended so perfectly for me where the handle went into the bow; or I come across where he'd scratched the threshing count on the barn door, with one of those clumsy fives of his in it; or it's time for someone to make the first move for bed; or some winter dusk when the sun's drawing water down beyond the frozen marshes—do you know that time of day? It's as if your heart slips into low gear.

(I'm glad Jeff can't hear me. But I don't know, maybe he wouldn't think it sounded soft. Just because he never *said* anything like that himself—you can't go by that.)

I always feel like telling something about him then. I don't know, if I can tell something to show people what he was really like it seems to help.

The wild goose flew over this evening. The sky was full of grey clouds. It looked as if it was worried about something. I could tell about Jeff and the wild goose. I never have.

It really started the afternoon before. We went hunting about four o'clock. I was fourteen and he was sixteen.

You'd never know we were brothers. You could tell exactly how he was going to look as a man, and I looked like a child that couldn't make up his mind *what* shape his face would take on later. He could lift me and my load (though he'd never once glance my way if I tackled anything beyond my strength—trying to lead a steer that was tough in the neck, or putting a cordwood butt on top of the pile, or anything). But I always seemed the older, somehow. He always seemed to—well, look up to me or something, it didn't matter how often I was mean to him.

I could draw the sprawling back field on a piece of paper and figure out the quickest way to mow it, by algebra; but when I took the machine out on the field itself I wouldn't know where to begin. Jeff could take one look at the field and know exactly where to make the first swath. That was the difference between us.

And I had a quick temper, and Jeff never lost his temper except when someone was mad at *me*.

I never saw him mad at me himself but that one day. The day was so still and the sun was so bright the leaves seemed to be breathing out kind of a yellow light before they fell to the ground. I always think there's something sort of lonesome about that, don't you?

I'm no kind of a hunter. You wouldn't think I was a country boy at all.

But Jeff was. He was a wonderful shot; and the minute he stepped into the woods there was a sort of brightness and a hush in his face together, I can't describe it. It wasn't that he liked the killing part. He seemed to have a funny kind of love and respect for whatever he hunted that I didn't have at all. If I don't see any game the first quarter mile I get to feel like I'm just walking around on a fool's errand, dragging a heavy gun along. But Jeff's spell never slacked for a second.

You'd have to live in the country to know what hunting meant to anyone like Jeff. And to know how he rated with the grown-up men; here's just this kid, see, and he knows right where to find the game, no matter how scarce it is, and to bring it home.

Anyway, we'd hardly gone any distance at all—we were just rounding that bend in the log road where there's the bit of open swamp and then what's left of the old back orchard, before the woods start—when Jeff halted suddenly and grabbed my arm.

"What's the matter?" I said.

I guess I spoke louder than ordinary, because I was startled. I hadn't thought of having to be cautious so soon.

Jeff's gun went up, but he didn't have time for even a chance shot. There was a flash of the big buck's flag. He'd been standing under the farthest apple tree. Then in a single motion, like the ripple in a rope when you hold one end in your hand and whap the other against the ground, he disappeared into the thicket.

Deer will sometimes stand and watch you for minutes, still as stone. Stiller than thunder weather. Stiller than holding your breath. So still you can't believe it. They're cocked for running, but you get the feeling they weren't there before you saw them.

Your eyes seem to have plucked them right out of the air. Their feet don't seem to quite rest on the ground.

But the second you speak, they're off. The human voice is like a trigger.

It would have been a sure shot for Jeff. There wasn't a twig between them. It would have been the biggest buck anyone had brought home that year. Even I felt that funny sag in the day that you get when game's been within your reach except for carelessness and now there's nothing. You just keep staring at the empty spot, as if you should have known that was the one place a deer would be.

Jeff turned to me. His eyes were so hot in his head I almost crouched.

"For God's sake," he said, "don't you know enough to keep your tongue still when you're huntin'?"

It was like a slap in the face.

The minute Jeff heard what he'd said the anger went out of him. But you'd have to live in the country to know what a funny feeling it left between us. For one hunter to tell another he'd spoiled a shot. It was as if you'd reminded someone to take off his cap inside the house.

I didn't say a word. Only in my mind. I seemed to hear my mind shouting, "You just wait. You'll see. I'll never . . . never. . . ." Never what, I didn't know—but just that never, never again. . . .

Jeff rumbled with a laugh, trying to put the whole thing behind us, as a joke.

"Well," he said, offhand like, "that one certainly moved fast didn't he? But we'll circle around. Maybe we'll ketch him in the choppin', what?"

I didn't say a word. I just broke down my gun and took out the cartridge, then and there. I put the cartridge into my windbreaker pocket and turned toward home.

"Ain't you comin'?" Jeff said.

"What d'ya *think*?" I said.

I glanced behind me when he'd gone on. I don't know, it always strikes me there's something sort of lonesome about seeing anyone walk away back-so. I almost changed my mind and ran and caught up with him.

But I didn't. I don't know why I could never smooth things over with Jeff right away when I knew he was sorry. I wanted to then, but I couldn't. I had to hang on to the hurt and keep it fresh. I hated what I was doing, but there it was.

It was pitch dark when Jeff got home that night, but he didn't have any deer.

I sort of kept him away from me all the next day. I hated myself for cutting off all his clumsy feelers to make up. ("What was the algebra question you showed the teacher how to do when you was only ten?") It always kind of gets me, seeing through what anyone is trying to do like that, when they don't know you can. But I couldn't help it.

(Once Jeff picked up about fifty bags of cider apples nights after school. The day he took them into town and sold them he bought every single one of us a present. I followed him to the barn that evening when he went to tend the horse. He didn't hear me coming. He was searching under the wagon seat and shaking out all the straw around the horse. He didn't want to tell me what he was looking for, but I made him. He'd lost a five dollar bill out of the money the man at the cider mill had given him. But he'd kept the loss to himself, not to spoil our presents. That's what he was like.)

It was just about dusk when Jeff rushed into the shop the day after I'd spoiled his shot at the deer. He almost never got so excited he forgot himself, like I did. But he was that way then.

"Git your gun, Kenny, quick," he said. "There's a flock o' *geese* lit on the marsh."

It would be hard to explain why that gave even me such a peculiar thrill. Wild geese had something—well, sort of mystic—about them.

When the geese flew south in the fall, high in the sky, people would run outdoors and watch them out of sight. And when they turned back to the house again they'd have kind of a funny feeling. The geese seemed to be about the most—distant, sort of—thing in the world. In every way. You couldn't picture them on the ground, like a normal bird. Years and years ago. Steve Hammond had brought one down, and it was still the first thing anyone told about him to a stranger. People said, "He shot a wild goose once," in the same tone they'd say of some famous person they'd seen, "I was close enough to touch him."

I was almost as excited as Jeff. But I kept rounding up my armful, pretending the geese didn't matter much to me one way or the other.

"Never mind the *wood*," Jeff said. He raced into the house for his gun.

I piled up a full load before I went into the house and dropped it into the box. It must have almost killed him to wait for me. But he did.

"Come on. Come on," he urged, as we started down across the field. "And put in a ball cartridge. We'll never git near enough fer shot to carry."

I could see myself hitting that small a target with a ball cartridge! But I did as he said.

When we got to the railroad cut, we crawled on our bellies, so we could use the embankment the rails ran along as a blind. We peeked over it, and there they were.

They were almost the length of the marsh away, way down in that mucky spot where the men cut sods for the dike, but their great white breasts looked big as pennants. They had their long black necks stretched up absolutely straight and still, like charmed cobras. They must have seen us coming down across the field.

Jeff rested the barrel of his gun on a rail. I did the same with mine. But mine was shaking so it made a clatter and I raised it higher.

"I'll count five," Jeff whispered. "Then both fire at once."

I nodded and he began to count.

"One. Two. Three. . . ."

I fired.

Jeff's shot came a split second afterward. He gave me a quick inquisitive glance, but he didn't say a word about me firing before the count was up.

He threw out his empty shell and loaded again. But the geese had already lifted, as if all at once some spring in the ground had shot them into the air. They veered out over the river.

All but one, that is. Its white breast was against the ground and we didn't see it in the blur of wings until its own wings gave one last flutter.

"We got one!" Jeff shouted. "Well, I'll be *damned*. We got one!"

He bounded down across the marsh. I came behind, walking.

When I got there he was stroking the goose's soft down almost tenderly. It was only a dead bird to me now, but to him it seemed like some sort of mystery made flesh and shape. There was hardly a mark on it. The bullet had gone through his neck, fair as a die.

Then Jeff made a funny face. He handed the goose to me. He was sort of grinning.

"Here," he said. "Carry her. She's yours. That was some shot, mister."

"Mine?" I said.

"Sure." He looked half sheepish. "I'm a hell of a hunter, I am. I had two ball cartridges in this here pocket, see, and two shot in this one." He put his hand into the first pocket and held out two ball cartridges in his palm. "I guess I got rattled and put the shot in my gun instidd o' the ball. You know how far shot'd carry. It was you that got him, no doubt about *that*."

I carried the goose home.

It didn't mean much to me, but he didn't know that. He could only go by what it would have meant to him, if he'd been the one to carry it home. I knew what he was thinking. This would wipe out what I'd done yesterday. And the men wouldn't look at me now the way they looked at a bookworm but the way they looked at a hunter.

I'm glad that for once I had the decency to pretend I was as excited and proud as he'd thought I'd be. I'm glad I didn't say a word—not then—to let him know I saw through the trick.

For I knew it was a trick. I knew I hadn't shot the goose. While he was counting I'd felt that awful passion to wreck things which always got into me when I was still smarting over something. I had fired before he did, on purpose. Way over their heads, to scare them.

The day Jeff went away we sort of stuck around close to each other, but we couldn't seem to find anything to say.

I went out to the road to wait for the bus with him. Jeff had on his good clothes. They never looked right on him. When I dressed up I looked different, but Jeff never did. I don't know why, but every time I saw Jeff in his good clothes I felt sort of—well, like *defending* him or something.

The bus seemed to take a long time coming. He was going away in the army. He'd be with the guys who were twice as much like him as I was, but just the same I knew he'd rather be with me than with them. I don't know, buses are such darned lonesome things, somehow.

When the bus was due, and I knew we only had left what few

minutes it might be late, I tried to think of something light to say, the way you're supposed to.

The only thing that came into my mind was that day with the goose. It was a funny thing to bring up all of a sudden. But now we were a couple of years older I thought I could make something out of it to amuse him. Besides, when someone's going away you have the feeling that you ought to get everything straight between you. You hardly ever can, but you get the feeling.

"You shot the goose that day," I said, "didn't you?"

He nodded.

I'd never have opened my fool mouth if I'd known what was going to happen then. I'd felt sort of still and bad, but I hadn't felt like crying. How was I to know that the minute I mentioned that day the whole thing would come back so darn plain? I'd have died rather than have Jeff see my face break up like that.

But on the other hand, I don't care how soft it sounds, I'm sort of glad I did, now. He didn't look embarrassed, to see me cry. He looked so darned surprised—and then all at once he looked happier than I believe I ever saw him.

That was Jeff. He'll never come back. I don't even know which Korean hill it was—the telegram didn't say. But when I tell anything about him like this I seem to feel that *somewhere* he's sort of, I don't know, half-smiling—like he used to when we had some secret between us we'd never even discussed. I feel that if I could just make him absolutely clear to everyone he wouldn't really be dead at all. Tonight when the geese flew over I wished I knew how to write a book about him.

The geese didn't light this time. They never have since that day. I don't know, I always think there's something lonesome about wild geese.

But I feel better now. Do you know how it is?

Long, Long After School

I ran into Wes Holman the very day I was collecting for Miss Tretheway's flowers. But it never came into my head to ask him for a contribution.

Miss Tretheway had taught Grade Three in our town for exactly fifty years. She had died the night before in her sleep. As chairman of the school board I had thought it would be fitting if all the Grade Three alumni who were still around made up enough money to get a really handsome "piece". She had no relatives. If I'd given it an instant's consideration I'd have known that Wes himself must have been in Grade Three some time or other; but I didn't.

Wes was just coming through the cemetery gate as I was going in Wes "looks after" the cemetery, and I sometimes take a short cut through it on my way to work. I should say that Wes is our local "character". His tiny house up behind the ball park is furnished with almost nothing but books, and he can quote anyone from Seneca to Henry James. But that's his job: caretaker-about-town.

When I spoke to him about Miss Tretheway, a curious change came into his face. You couldn't say that he turned pale, but his stillness was quite different from the conventional one on such occasions. I had expected him to come out with some quote or other, but he didn't say a word.

He didn't go to her funeral. But he sent her flowers of his own. Or brought them, rather. The following day, when I took the short cut again, I surprised him on his knees placing them.

His little bunch of flowers was the most incongruous thing you could imagine. It was a corsage. A corsage of simple flowers, such as a young boy sends his girl for her first formal dance. And more incongruous than its presence in the circumstance of death was its connection with Miss Tretheway herself. I'm quite sure that Miss Tretheway never once had a beau send her flowers, that she'd never been to a dance in her whole life.

I suppose it would never have occurred to me to question anyone but Wes about his motive for doing a thing like that. But I asked Wes about it with no thought of rudeness whatever. Wes's privacy seemed to be everyone's property. There was probably a little self-conscious democracy in the gesture when we talked to him at all.

"She was so beautiful," he answered me, as if no other explanation was needed.

That was plainly ridiculous. That Miss Tretheway was a fine person for having spent a lifetime in small, unheralded services could not be disputed—but obviously she hadn't *ever* been beautiful. Her sturdy plainness was never transfigured, not even for an instant, by the echo of anything winsomer which had faded. Her eyes had never been very blue, her skin very pink, or her hair very brown. She wasn't very anything. Her heart might have been headlong (I think now that it was), but there was always that curious precision and economy in her face which lacks altogether the grain of helter-skelter necessary to any kind of charm. In short, even when she'd been a girl, she'd been the sort of girl whose slightest eagerness, more than if she were ugly or old, a young man automatically shies away from.

"But, Wes," I said, half-joking, "she wasn't beautiful. What made you say that?"

His story went something like this. He told it with a kind of dogged, confessional earnestness. I guess he'd come to figure that whenever we asked him a personal question he might as well satisfy our curiosity completely, first as last.

"Perhaps you remember how the kids used to tease me at school," he said. (I didn't. I guess those things stick in your mind according to which end of the teasing you happen to be on.) "If the boys would be telling some joke with words in it to giggle over, they'd look at me and say, 'Shhhh . . . Wes is blushing.' Or if we were all climbing up the ladder to the big beam in Hogan's stable, they'd say 'Look at Wes. He's so scared he's turning pale.' Do you remember the night you steered your sled into mine, going down Parker hill?"

"No," I said. "Did I do it on purpose?"

"I don't know," Wes said. "Maybe you didn't I thought you did."

Maybe I did. I don't remember.

"I was taking Mrs. Banks's wash home on my sled, and you were coasting down the hill. The basket upset and all the things fell out on the snow. Don't you remember . . . Miss Tretheway came along and you all ran. She helped me pick up the stuff and shake the snow off it. She went with me right to Mrs. Banks's door and told her what had happened. I could never have made Mrs. Banks believe *I* didn't upset the stuff myself."

"I'm sorry," I said. I probably *had* done it on purpose.

"That's all right," he said. "I didn't mind the boys so much. It was the girls. You can't hit a girl. There just wasn't anything I could do about the girls. One day Miss Tretheway was showing us a new game in the school yard. I don't remember exactly how it went, but that one where we all made a big circle and someone stood in the centre. I put my hand out to close up the ring with the biggest Banks girl, but she wouldn't take it. She said, 'Your hands are dirty.' Miss Tretheway made us both hold out our hands. She said, 'Why, Marilyn, Wes's hands are much cleaner than yours. Maybe Wes doesn't like to get *his* hands dirty, did you ever think about that?' She took Marilyn's place herself. Her hand felt safe and warm, I remember . . . and I guess that's the first day I thought she was beautiful."

"I see," I said.

I did, and yet I didn't. The Wes I remembered would hate anything with the suggestion of teacher's pet about it. The only Wes I could seem to remember was the Wes of adolescence: the tough guy with the chip on his shoulder.

He was coming to that. But he stuck in an odd parenthesis first.

"Did you ever notice Miss Tretheway," he said, "when . . . well, when the other teachers would be talking in the hall about the dances they'd been to over the weekend? Or when she'd be telling some kid a story after school and the kid would run off right in the middle of a sentence when she saw her mother coming to pick her up?"

"No," I said. "Why? What about it?"

"Oh, nothing, I guess." He drew a deep breath. "Anyway, I decided I'd be stronger and I'd study harder than anyone. And I was, wasn't I? I did. Do you remember the year they voted me the best all-round student in High School?" (I didn't. It must have been after I'd graduated.) "I guess I just can't remember how happy I was about that. I guess I was so happy I could believe anything. That must have been why I let the boys coax me into going to the closing dance." He smiled. "I thought since they'd voted for me . . . but you can't legislate against a girl's glance."

Those were his exact words. Maybe he'd read them somewhere. Maybe they were his own. I don't know. But it was the
kind of remark which had built up his quaint reputation as the
town philosopher.

"I didn't want to go out on the dance floor," he said. "I'd
never danced a foxtrot or anything. The girls all had on their
evening dresses, and somehow they looked different altogether.
They looked as if they wouldn't recognize *themselves* in their day
clothes. Anyway, the boys grabbed hold of me and made me get
into a Paul Jones. I was next to Toby Wenford in the big ring. Jane
Evans was right opposite me when the music stopped, but she
danced with Toby instead—and the girl next *to* Jane just glanced
at me and then went and sat down. I guess it was a pretty foolish
thing to do, but I went down in the basement and drove my fist
through a window."

"Is that the scar?" I said. I couldn't think of anything else to
say.

"Oh, it was a lot worse than that," he said. He pulled up his
sleeve and traced the faint sickle of the scar way up his arm. "You
can hardly see it now. But I almost bled to death right there. I
guess I might have, if it hadn't been for Miss Tretheway."

"Oh?" I said. "How's that?"

"You see, they didn't have any plasma around in bottles
then," he said, "and in those days no one felt too comfortable
about having his blood siphoned off. I guess no one felt like taking
any chances for me, anyway. Mother said I could have hers, but
hers wasn't right. Mine's that odd type—three, isn't it? Miss
Tretheway's was three, too . . . and that's funny, because only
seven percent of people have it. She gave me a whole quart, just
as soon as she found out that hers would match."

"I see," I said. So that was it. And yet I had a feeling that that
wasn't it—not quite.

"She used to come see me every day," he said. "She used to
bring me books. Did you know that books . . . well, that for
anyone like me that's the only way you can . . . ?" He hesitated,
and I knew that that wasn't quite it either.

Not until he spoke again, when he spoke so differently, was I
sure that only now was he coming to the real thing.

"Do you know what Miss Tretheway said when I thanked her
for the transfusion?" he said. "She made a joke of it. She said: 'I
didn't know whether an old maid's blood would be any good to a
fine young specimen like you, Wes, or not.' The thing I always

remember, I knew that was the first time she'd ever called herself an old maid to anyone, and really felt like laughing. And I remember what *I* said. I said: 'Miss Tretheway, you're making me blush.' And do you know, that was the very first time I'd ever been able to say *that*, and laugh, myself."

There was quite a long silence.

"She was beautiful," he added softly. "She was a real lady."

The cemetery is right next to the river. I looked down the river where the cold December water lapped at the jagged ice thrown up on the banks, and I thought about a boy the colour of whose skin was such that he could never blush, and I thought about a girl who had never been asked to a dance. I thought about the corsage. My curiosity was quite satisfied. But somehow I myself had never felt less beautiful, or less of a gentleman.

Cleft Rock,
With Spring

Madge Kendall took off her earrings and dropped them wearily into the tray on her dresser. It had promised to be a good party: the Pattersons were the kind of hosts who have a way of sparking you into a true party blitheness the moment they take your coat. But once more she'd brought home with her that odd sense of frustration. Jeff never used to act like that.

When Ken Patterson had said, "What makes you so quiet, Madge?" Jeff had said. "Oh, my wife is just bottling up her emotions. We use them for conserves in the winter. They have a flavour rather like quince." The tone, if not the words, had been almost derisive.

Not that Jeff was a smarty. His face corrected that. And if he were merely a smarty, the others would snub him. They wouldn't repeat him with the generosity they did.

Yet even when he was the hub of the party, he didn't seem to be satisfied. There was something hectic about his behaviour.

And lately there was a new edginess in the glibbest of his

remarks. "You should see Madge whipping my Agatha Christie under a cushion when her artistic friends call. You see, she knows this character with a superb talent for writing unpublished mood pieces—and a radio actor that says 'straw'bris, black'bris. . . .' "

Did the stubborn drive that had brought him, a village boy with a genius for figures, all the way from office clerk to chief actuary in eight short years and to more money than she'd ever been used to herself, explain it? Was that drive restless for new fields, now he knew he had his job—*and* his wife—in the hollow of his hand?

Or had it turned his head to have the strange women at parties like these almost invariably point out to him how much he looked like Laurence Olivier?

"And I'm only the poor man's Claudette Colbert," she'd said tonight. The rest had laughed, because it did describe her own rather plaintive looks so accurately. But Jeff hadn't even smiled. He seemed to resent her scoring anything that approached an applaudable remark.

He was taking out his cufflinks, with the same apathetic gestures as she. They didn't discuss the party. That's the worse sign of all, she thought: when you don't post mortem parties any more.

They never did now. That was the funny part: the moment they were alone, their own talk lapsed into a crippling matter-of-factness, like the talk of two people who have to keep skirting some sensitive topic.

She got into bed, but she couldn't sleep. She didn't understand him any more. You'd think it was he, not she, who was the city product. She felt shrunken, for being forever made conscious of her mediocrity.

He didn't use to be like that. He never used to have that relentless obsession to show her how totally he could eclipse her.

It was her suggestion that they take this trip back home. To Dondale. The village where he'd been brought up, and where she had spent her childhood summers. With her mother's widowed sister, who had insisted that the company of simple village children would be the best formative experience possible for Madge. Those were the years when types like Aunt Emily fancied it terribly smart to refurbish an old mill like the one in Dondale and live in it through July and August.

Madge's desire for this visit now had something to do with the idea, persistent against all contradictions of experience, that

127

reviving an original happiness is as simple as going back to the original scene of it.

They were staying at the small hotel in town, but Dondale was near enough that they could go back and forth every day.

Now, driving along the dusty road to the old picnic lake, this first noon, she was sorry they had come.

It was that hot, dry summer.

She had known that Jeff's family had moved away and scattered. That there were strangers living in his old house. That the old mill house had burned down—tramps, they suspected. And that any friends still here would be much older. She hadn't been naive enough not to know that you can never go home again, in that sense.

But it had never occurred to her that a place itself could age.

Dondale looked like a faded snapshot of itself. It seemed to her that the parched alders, their leaves crumbling away from the veining inside, were creeping in closer around the fields. And in the fields the grass reminded her of ribbon grass she'd seen one time, with a couple of peacock feathers, inside a vase in an unused parlour. They always planted ribbon grass on graves.

Around the bend beyond the long dusty hill below the church and the houses, and past the meadow where the rocks showed crusted with parched moss in the bed of the dry brook, they came upon a man and a span of horses. The man sprang upright on his load at the sound of the motor. He was so busy reining his horses to the exact edge of the narrow road that he didn't look their way at all.

But as they squeezed by, Madge caught a glimpse of his face in the rear-view mirror.

"Jeff," she exclaimed, "do you know who I think that was? That was Dave Woodworth!"

He braked the car. "That's what I thought," he said. "Do you want to stop?"

"Well, of course!" she said. And then she hesitated. "No," she said, "never mind. We're too far by now."

Everything had changed so, what would there be to say?

They ate lunch in the old pine grove by the lake. The pines had grown so tall they seemed now to belong more to the air than to the earth, and the warnings of fire hazard tacked to them seemed to annul their old intimacy. The lake was so low that huge rocks were exposed in the shallows where they used to swim. The water had a sweetish, withdrawn smell.

After lunch, it wasn't as it used to be. As soon as the dishes were packed, it seemed as if they were waiting to leave.

They sauntered up and down the road in either direction. The flying grasshoppers swivelled as if on a single axle in the dust, and the locusts spun the dry heat in their piercing monotone. It was like those walks you try to soak up the wait between trains with, in a strange city: when they got back hardly any time had gone.

They sat down, finally, on two rocks by the beach. Staring steadily at the hypnotic lap of the waves until they seemed to be floating too. They began to say, "Do you remember the time we . . . ?"

Yet it seemed to her that they were doing even this doggedly. The images they dredged up wouldn't quite come clear. The dimension of spontaneity was missing.

"You know what we forgot?" she said. "Some drinking water. I'm thirsty. I never thought of bringing water here, did you?"

"No," he said. "Coals to Newcastle. But I'm thirsty too. Do you feel like walking as far as the old mill brook? There must be water there, surely."

But there wasn't. It too was dry. Jeff threw out his hands in a gesture of resignation.

"Well," he said, "I guess that's that. Do you want to start back to town?"

"Oh, no," Madge protested, "not just yet." She didn't know why, but it seemed important that they musn't give this day up until they absolutely had to.

"Didn't there use to be a spring . . . ?" Jeff said suddenly.

"Yes!" she said. "The spring! *I* remember."

"Let's see," he said. "We used to go back that old log road and. . . ."

They didn't really think they'd find it. The log road was so grown up, and they couldn't remember how far back the spring had been, or on which side.

So that when they both heard it at once they stopped short. Jeff motioned excitedly for silence, as if they had been stalking a timid animal.

The spring was exactly the same as ever: starting somewhere in the root cavern of the same blown-up log, falling down the slight bank, and spending itself in the ferns. The ferns grew fresh and green all around it. The water ran clean and cool.

It seemed as unchanged as the huge cleft boulder it had always splashed against.

"Imagine!" she said. "After all this drought."

"Like love, eh?" Jeff said, with a flash of his hectic party levity that gave her a sudden chill. "*Ne*-ver parches, *ne*-ver parches . . . I'll go get a cup."

Madge ignored the first part of his speech. "A cup?" she said. "In Dondale? Make a birch dipper, for heaven's sake."

"I don't know if I remember how."

But he located a birch tree and he made a conical bark dipper as expertly as ever.

He filled it with water and held it toward her, leaning across the boulder.

"Just a second," she said. She too was leaning against the boulder, extricating a sharp twig from one of her shoes.

Jeff set the tip of the dipper into the fissure that divided the rock, absently tilting it this way and that until its equilibrium was stable.

Suddenly he stood upright.

"It couldn't be!" he said.

"What couldn't be?"

"Come look."

Madge put her hands to the sides of her face and peered down into the deep cleft of the boulder.

Jeff pointed. "There."

"Of course," she said softly.

It was a crude ring. They used to make them by bending an ox-shoe nail into a circle. A child's imagination could easily transform the square head of the nail into a precious stone.

"Do you remember?" Jeff said.

Madge nodded. She remembered all right. It was the day's first distinct image.

"Do you know," she said, "I came back later that afternoon and tried and tried to fish it out with a long stick? But just when I'd get it almost to the top it'd slip back. I cried."

"You cried?" he exclaimed. "And who threw it there? You threw it there yourself, didn't you?"

"I know I threw it there," Madge said. "And you know why. You had to spoil everything."

I've been picturing it all wrong, she thought—he was never any different. A touch of anger sharpened her voice.

"Don't you remember? You were just fitting the ring onto my finger when some other kid came along—wasn't it Dave, actually? It *was* Dave—and you said, 'Maybe an ox-nail ring won't be fancy enough for Madge to wear, I guess we'd better take it home and put it in the pig's nose.' You had to turn the whole thing into one of your infernal wisecracks. For Dave's benefit. You're always doing something like that with me the minute you have an audience."

"For Dave's benefit?" Jeff said. "For Dave's benefit?"

He spoke almost involuntarily. The way you do in one of those moments when deliberate misrepresentations have reached the challenging point where, no matter what, they just can't be allowed to stand uncorrected.

"Now let's not twist things around. Since when have I ever done anything for anyone's benefit, as you put it, but yours? And it gets me exactly as far as it did that day."

"Jeff," Madge said, "now you know you. . . ."

"This is what I know," he said. "Just let me finish. And listen carefully. Because, as they say, I can only give you the answer once." He paused. "I remember you had a 'boughten' dress on. . . ."

For some reason, that picture brought a flash of anger into his voice too and a kind of stumbling fluency.

"You were just *sitting* there, with your . . . crisp . . . boughten . . . city . . . dress on. You never had to make any effort whatsoever . . . about anything . . . to be . . . well, automatically ahead of me. You knew you were city-grained and I was homemade. . . ."

He glanced at her, bristling against possible interruption, but she didn't interrupt.

"You know"—he seemed to slip into the present tense without noticing it—"that no matter how I go you one better in your own field—money . . . cultchah . . . or you name it, I'll try it—no matter how I knock myself out trying to impress you, I can never catch up on that head start of yours. All you have to do is let your . . . entrenchment? *I* don't know what the word is . . . sit back and smile."

He looked at her again, challenging her to interrupt, but she didn't say a word.

"I'm not one damn bit ashamed of being homemade, mind you. But you wouldn't understand. I remember one day I was

131

trying to swing the scythe and my older brother came along and smiled at me. All you have to do is look at me, just look at me, and I get that. . . ."

He broke off all at once, suddenly self-conscious, and pointed to the dipper.

"All right," he said. "Were you thirsty, or weren't you?"

Madge put the dipper to her lips, and the touch of the cool water stopped their trembling. She felt a release as spilling as when some chance paragraph in a book you pick up defines exactly the way you are feeling right then.

But she took a long time drinking. Because she knew she must be very careful about choosing the next words she spoke. Because she felt as peculiarly shamed—though it was not for anything like exactly the same reasons—as if she'd been guilty of keeping her distance from a child who'd been trying to engage her with an approach he wasn't any too sure of himself. Or of surprising him, in the very presence of others to whom he was making some innocent boast, with the reminder that she'd actually been there when the thing happened.

Jeff looked about him nervously.

"Whenever you're through," he said, holding his hand toward the dipper. "I'd like to rinse off my own tongue." Trying to cover up. Trying to put his instantly regretted confession behind them, beyond reference.

And then he said quickly, "How would you like to stop and see old Dave on the way back?"

She knew then what she must say, for his desperate pride's sake. She knew all she must say, for now. Later they would get it all straight, but not now.

"I'd love to see old Dave," she said. "And thanks, darling, for trying to give your little city mouse such a terrific build-up. For a minute there you almost had me convinced."

"But you *are* . . ." he began.

"Shush!" she said. "Or you will have me believing it. And fish me out my ring."

Glance in
the Mirror

He was right on the verge of capturing it exactly, just before she came into the study. And that was wonderful.

They thought that writing was always wonderful, but most of the time it was the loneliest job in the world. That crippling stillness when you sat down to try the first few lines. As if everything you looked at was tensed for you to make a sound and you were tongue-tied, like someone in a nightmare. If that lasted long enough you would sit there then and hear the sound of your own life going by. A lifetime is not forever, and yours was already half gone. You would think of all the other times you'd sat here alone, while the rest were building something tangible. Together. Really together with the real thing, not this shadow of it. The laughing and the touching and the joining with the same thoughts. . . . It wasn't wonderful then.

Then maybe it would begin to come. In a gathering rush. Like the coursing of blood through a vein again after thumb pressure has been relaxed. You could seem to hear the voices of everything, all at once. You would have words for the touch of flesh, and words for the way of two people who were really together, and words for the wordlessness in the mouths of people who had never had anyone, and words for all the incommunicable shadows on the heart that the face hid—the morning ones of love and hope and being young, and the still afternoon ones of failure and of someone gone away and of growing old. . . . And time itself could be caught and said.

And *then* you'd sit there and feel what it's like when a man first knows that he's done only bits of the thing that it was meant for him to do wholly. And again just one word would pulse in your brain: alone . . . alone . . . alone. . . .

But it could be wonderful. Like now. The day when there would be a single thing to fasten on. A thing that had been cloudy and coreless inside you, like an ache; but you hadn't given up, and now you read the words, there it was, almost exactly in the shape you could see it must have, and *outside* you.

Then it would seem that you could possess anything whatever, by telling it. That nothing would be intolerable if you could find words for it. Time was not a fear any more and loneliness was beaten. Then you were free like no one else. You wouldn't exchange places with anyone.

He was reading over what he had written, when she opened the door.

Her name was Anna. And they were really together. That is possible. It doesn't happen with everyone, and to those who have never known it, time makes a steady sound like a far-off bell. But it happened with them. And they knew it. And it was wonderful. It was an over-all thing like the quiet song of health or the subtle mending of sleep . . . to have your voice come back to you, not in its own thin echo, but with the edges gone as if with the smoothing and softening of fire-light, because another had heard it exactly.

Her name was Anna, and it meant a face . . . and the inimitable safety. The great sweet wonderful safety from the cry of things not understood, and things said and things not said, and things done and things not done, and the sound of time and the sound of time gone by. . . .

She came in, and he saw her glance at the mirror, instinctively, before she spoke. She took off her hat and ran her fingers through her curly, close-cropped, wheat-coloured hair. He caught the clean fragrance coming from it, like a breath.

Then she came over and sat down in the chair next his desk and lit a cigarette, frowning a little at the first inhalation of smoke. Then she smiled at him, a long settled smile, as if she were all ready to talk.

Her name was not Anna. Her name was Sheila, and she was his wife.

He felt everything leave him, the instant she came into the room. He turned the sheet back on the roller, faking a correction.

"How's it going, darling?" she said.

"Terrible."

"Oh, you always say that." She laughed. "You're so serious about it, Jeff. You know it really isn't a matter of life and death, darling. . . ."

I don't suppose it is, he thought . . . to anyone else. I don't suppose I should expect her to understand that.

"Let me see it," she said. 'I'll bet it's wonderful."

"It's terrible," he said.

He took the paper out of the typewriter and tore it lengthwise and crosswise very thoroughly and dropped it into the waste basket.

"Jeff," she said, "I think you're mean. You never let me see anything you write lately. Why do you have to be so darn secret about it? Honestly, you'd think it was something I'd *caught* you at."

It's funny, he thought, the way she can hit it right on the head like that sometimes.

He didn't speak, and she said, "Jeff, could the reason be that you don't love me?"

Oh no, he thought, it's nothing as simple as that. Just the hint of a wry smile twitched his lips: and I suppose some people believe that I married her for her money . . . that it's as simple as *that*. He shook his head.

"I love you all right," he said.

"And I love you too, darling, believe me," she said eagerly. "That's why I wish you'd let me help you."

"Okay," he said. "Go ahead. Help me."

"Well," she said, "not so much with the writing, maybe. . . . But to tell the truth, darling, I don't think you ought to be writing at all. You should be doing something else. You sweat and fuss and get all steamed up and it's got to be *just* so." She laughed tolerantly, but incredulously. "And what *difference* does it make? You're wasting your whole life puttering around with a few old words, and what difference do they make?"

That's nice, he thought, that's very nice, to hear someone else say that.

"What else could I do?" he said. "I'm not a kid any more."

"Oh, there are lots of things to do. For instance, if you'd just be sensible about this money business, Jeff—I don't understand you . . . if you'd just let me give you a *start* in something, some business or something. . . ."

He didn't say anything.

"First," she said, as if it were already settled, "we'll take a nice long trip and get this old stuff right out of your head. We'll go to Gaspé and Banff and the Cabot Trail and oh I don't know where, and get all those stuffy old words right out of your head. Like the sound of that? Eh?"

135

"I don't think so," he said. "I'm sorry."

"It's because I said it would be my treat, isn't it? Jeff, you're so darn silly. . . ."

"But you just said you bet what I was writing was wonderful. You say everything I write is wonderful."

"Of course it's wonderful, silly." She said it quite sincerely, with no consciousness of self-contradiction whatever. "I just meant. . . ."

"Maybe you meant it didn't bring in much cash."

"I didn't mean that at all. You're so darn silly about money. I mean, it doesn't bring in much money, really, does it . . . but I certainly don't worry about that. It isn't as if I had to depend on. . . . I'm sorry, darling," she interrupted herself, "I didn't really mean it like that."

"That's all right," he said.

What is it, he thought, this business of loving someone that particular way? They say it isn't love at all. But it is. It's not the flesh, wholly. The little shock whenever our hands touch even now, some of it is that perhaps, but not all of it.

What is this business of the flesh, anyway? She's not really beautiful. I can understand why another man might not find her so, and yet with what part of me would I find such blindness on his part incredible? What is this business of the single face? There are women who resemble her almost exactly. You'd think the feeling for them would be almost exactly the same as the feeling for her. But it isn't. It's so different it's a different *kind* of thing.

Why *is* it that I can forget her when I'm alone, but that the instant she comes into the room she brings the love and the destruction both?

And then suddenly he felt the warmth creeping back. If I could just get that outside me, he thought. . . .

She glanced at her watch. "Heavens!" she exclaimed, "I didn't know it was so late . . . the time goes so quickly when I'm with you, darling, aren't you flattered? . . . I told Helen I'd pick her up at five and we'd look in on that art show at the Museum, although Lord knows I might as well try to read a page of Gaelic. . . . Would you like to come?"

"No, thanks," he said.

He put a fresh sheet of paper into the typewriter and wrote the title, THE SUMMER'S GONE.

"Have you got something?" she said.

"I think so."

"Good," she said. "Good luck with it." She picked up her hat and went over to the mirror. "And darling," she added lightly, as if it might have been the weather they'd been discussing before, "you don't mind anything I said, *do* you. I didn't mean to discourage you, or anything, you know that. If you want to go on trying I think that's wonderful. It's just wonderful."

He was writing quickly.

She had close-cropped hair, soft as a kitten's, and her skin was soft and smelled nice because she had always been rich and had never had any of the thoughts so sharp they gouge the skin a little too. The always having of money was in her, integrally, like a feature. Her face was fine, and it gave him that wonderful feeling which nothing but another face can, if it's the right one, and he loved her, but they were never really together.

She didn't know the way of any kind of silence. Silences were something she ran away from. The long safe silence of being together with someone was something she didn't know at all.

He realized that, but it didn't help anything. He didn't blame her. It was no one's fault. But she was destroying him. A writer is alone. A watcher is always alone. Yet if he has someone to be alone with, then his voice is sure and strong with the speaking which only the voices of the lonely can ever know.

But they were not together at all. She could destroy his voice, without knowing it, because she couldn't enter into any of the things that were his. He would feel a sort of shame he couldn't help for any part of his own way which was different from hers, and a deeper shame for the shame itself. If you build bridges, and a thing like that happens, you can go on building good bridges in spite of it. But if you are a writer. . . .

She was still in front of the mirror.

"Why, darling," she said, "listen to you. You're going like a house on fire. May I read it before I go? Please . . . just this once?"

Okay, he thought defiantly, go ahead, look in this mirror for a change. Just this minute he felt that wonderful free feeling again.

She took the sheet from him and began to read.

"Darling,"—she laughed suddenly—"her hair's like mine." She glanced in the mirror. "I'll bet you were thinking of *my* hair. I think you're sweet."

She put the paper down after a few more sentences, and lit a cigarette. Then she picked the paper up again and read it through quickly. She passed it back to him.

He looked at her, penitent already. Hoping there would be anger, and not hurt, on her face. But there was neither. Just a puzzled look and a mild amusement.

"It's wonderful, darling," she said. "I think it's wonderful. But why do you always have to make them so *grim?*" She laughed again. "Why don't you ever write one about you and me?"

She kissed him quickly, smiling, and went out the door.

He sat there, alone again, with that look of total abdication about his hands like the look you see in the face of someone on whom a joke has been sprung so dismaying that he doesn't know whether to laugh or cry.

He watched her walk down the path.

And then slowly his face began to change. For some reason, watching her through a window, walking away from him, so defencelessly back-to, so vulnerably small with distance, he was assaulted by an overwhelming tenderness toward her which he had never felt in his life before.

He reached for another piece of paper and put it into the typewriter for yet one more draft.

She loved him completely, no matter what he said or did, there was no doubt about that. And in her own way, she was absolutely unselfish. She would give him anything she had. In her own way, too, she tried *to understand and help him. Had he ever tried, really tried, to understand her at all? And how could he expect her to understand anyone as selfish and egotistic as a writer—who could never see that his few stuffy old words were less important than* any *kind of love . . . ?*